Toys in the Dust

A Leighton Jones Novel

First published in 2019 by Bloodhound Books

www.bloodhoundbooks.com

Print ISBN 978-1-912986-07-1

Also by NM Brown

The Girl On The Bus
Carpenter Road

For my wife…

Note: These events take place ten years before *Carpenter Road* and twenty years before *The Girl on the Bus*

Prologue

Tina Blanchette let the battered screen door clatter shut behind her as she carefully made her way down the four white stone stairs leading from the porch to the yard. She had to move slowly and watch each step because she was carrying her favourite Barbie doll and a selection of well-used accessories, including a yellow plastic poodle on a small lead.

At age seven, Tina desperately wanted to have had a real dog of her own just like her cousin Theo had, but because her mom said they couldn't – owing to the size of their modest home – having a pretend pet for Barbie was the next best thing. Tina had got it last Christmas and had slept with it beneath her pillow ever since. The dog even came with a small pink feeding bowl and a tiny plastic bone, but Tina never took those things outside when she was playing in her own or Suzy's neighbouring yard. They were simply too small, and she had learned from experience that small things could be easily lost among the tangled blades of grass.

Tina's modest home was located in a small cluster of sun-bleached houses which flanked a long ribbon of road between Oceanside and Barstow. Most of the buildings were single storey bungalows painted in muted pastel colours.

As Tina stepped away from her home, the heat on that afternoon made the road appear to ripple as if it was being viewed through a rainy window. But there was no rain here – just heat and dust. The sky above her was clear and the Californian air was tinged with the sweet muskiness of the wildfires that had been plaguing the San Diego area all summer. Tina secretly really liked the smell in the air – it reminded her of a time when her dad had still been around and he made a bonfire on the beach; Tina's mom, hated the smell. She moaned that it seeped into the clean washing.

Having safely navigated the steps, Tina – wearing a pair of faded jean shorts and an orange T-shirt – hurried past two other houses and eventually stopped outside a front yard where a slightly smaller girl was sitting on the parched ground playing intently with a similar doll to Tina's.

'Hey Suzy,' Tina said as she pushed through the creaking wooden gate in the waist high wall that hemmed in the small dusty yard.

'Hi,' Suzy said without looking up from the complicated pleat she was tying in the golden hair of her own plastic doll. Suzy was dressed in jean dungarees and had three streaks of white sunscreen on her face. It was a bit like war paint.

'Look what my Aunt Joan gave me,' Suzy said as she pointed one small hand towards the steps of her own porch where a large cardboard box sat on the bottom step.

'What is it?' Tina asked.

'A bunch of my cousin's old toys,' Suzy said indifferently. 'But some of them are busted,' she added with a dismissive shrug of her shoulders. 'Last year she gave me Mousetrap but most of the pieces were broken and nobody could fix it. We just threw it in the trashcan. My mom said Aunt Joan could've done that herself.'

Whilst Suzy concentrated on twisting the strands of synthetic hairs together, Tina stepped across the parched lawn to examine the mysterious arrival. Somebody had used a red marker pen to scrawl the name *Jackie* – Suzy's mother – on the side of the box.

'Wow,' there's lots of stuff here,' Tina said as she began rummaging through the variety of brightly coloured plastic objects.

'I know,' Suzy said without turning around. 'My mom brought it back from Reno last night. She said that because some bits are broken, she doesn't want me to take them all into the house.'

'Why?' Tina asked.

'She says we have enough junk of our own already. I've to take what I want, then the rest is going in the trash.'

'Hey, look at this!' Tina called.

Suzy glanced up to see her friend proudly holding a pink plastic speedboat with white seats and some neon coloured stickers decorating the sides. Tina was grinning as she turned the toy over and displayed it like a miniature TV game show hostess.

'It's a proper Barbie Wet n Wild boat! I've seen these before in *Toys R Us*, but my mom said they were too expensive. She always says that. We could put both of our dolls into it and sail them around.'

'I already thought about that,' Suzy said with a small shrug of her shoulders, 'but my mom's cleaning the upstairs of the house, and she's put bleach down in the bathtub.'

Tina frowned and thought for a moment. She didn't have a tub in her own home, only an erratic shower that went from freezing to burning in a matter of seconds. After chewing on her bottom lip for a moment, she formed an idea.

'What about your blow-up pool,' she suggested, 'the red one you had out in the yard at Easter?'

Suzy shook her head. 'That got snagged on a nail in the cellar and ripped along one side. My dad tried to patch it with some sticky black stuff but it didn't work and all the air came out again just slower.'

Tina sighed and turned the boat over in her hands for a moment. It seemed like her fantasy of the dolls riding across the waves was slipping away from her.

'I know!' Tina said. 'We could go across the road to the creek. It rained last week and there's probably still some water there.' The creek in question was a small dusty valley not too far from the girls' homes. Tina was, however, mistaken in her recollection. What she had thought had been rain on her bedroom window the previous week had only been spray from her mother's garden hose as she washed the thick grim off her car.

'Sure,' Suzy shrugged, 'but we can only go across there for a little while – my mom's still to fix lunch some.'

Having hastily gathered the dolls, boat and a matching plastic picnic table together, the two girls left Suzy's yard and wandered amiably along the roadside. The sun was even hotter as the two small girls drifted away from the protective shadow of the houses, towards the small area of colourless trees.

Their journey was a brief one. About a quarter of a mile along the baked road was an unofficial parking area. It was generally only used by contractors stopping for lunch, or for teenagers looking for somewhere quiet to make out. The ground in that location was littered with crushed fast food wrappers. In a few places, fragments of smashed beer bottles glinted on the ground like emeralds. Tina and Suzy stepped carefully through this minefield and crossed to the narrow dirt track, which wound like a serpent down into the small valley known locally as *the creek*. This was little more than a deep gash in the landscape where the runoff from occasional rainfall would collect, creating a temporary stream, until it eventually drained away into the sandy earth. On that particular afternoon it had been five months since the last rainfall, and the creek was arid and lifeless.

As the two girls knelt on the edge of the dry riverbed poking sticks in the cracked mud, they were both startled by a strange voice coming from behind and above them.

'Why, hello there.'

The girls turned to see a tall stranger standing on the rise of ground overlooking the creek. He was dressed in jeans and a faded T-shirt which hung on his scrawny frame like clothes on a scarecrow. As he picked his way down towards them, his feet kicked up small clouds of dust like puffs of smoke.

Eventually, he arrived by the side of the two small girls and crouched down to their level. Although she was too young to articulate it, Tina sensed that he was too close.

'Wow, you two girls are certainly having a good time,' he grinned at them, looking gleefully from one small face to another. 'Is this a new game, you guys are playing?' the stranger asked.

'No, we play this all the time,' Suzy said as she squinted to see a face in the silhouetted figure. The stranger wore metal glasses that reminded Suzy of the ones her great-grandma had worn before she died. He was also wearing a red baseball cap from which tufts of blond hair poked out. Something about the hair seemed familiar to Suzy.

Grinning widely, he shifted his legs and sat fully down on the dusty ground beside the two of them.

'What are you doing?' Tina asked. It didn't seem right for a grown-up to suddenly be there interfering in their game of Barbie dolls, but the stranger seemed unfazed by her question, he just smiled at her. There was something familiar about the stranger too, as if he had somehow been there before.

'I just thought I could join in your game. I love to play,' he said. 'When I was a kid my sister had such an amazing doll's house - with electric lights and everything. But she never let me play with it, or with any of the dolls.'

'That's not fair!' Suzy said. 'My brother is like that with all his Sega games.'

'Yeah, it made me feel really sad and left out.' The stranger's shoulders slumped down as he looked in sad recollection at the dusty ground. He reminded Tina of a stray dog she had once seen, hanging around the trash cans on collection day. Despite her mom's instruction to stay away from the dog, Tina had snuck out through the screen door and tried to give some Oreo cookies to the scrawny animal. She had crouched down nearby and held out a small hand, but the dog had snarled at her revealing curled teeth that were long and sharp.

'Hey,' he said, suddenly brightening up. 'It's a pity I don't have my own doll, that way I could play with you guys properly.'

Both girls nodded solemnly.

'By the way, I like your tattoo,' he said, looking at the cracked Tinkerbell on the back of Tina's hand.

There was a moment of silence, in which the stranger held his chin and frowned as if deep in thought. Then eventually his eyes widened in excitement.

'I don't suppose… No that would be silly.' He shook his head and looked his feet.

'What?' Suzy asked with a note of concern in her voice.

'I don't suppose either of you two ladies has an extra doll at home?' he asked with hopeful expression.

'I've only got one,' Tina said, softly. It wasn't true but at some level she could not yet comprehend, she was uncomfortable in the presence of this unusual and dominating stranger. Part of her hoped that if there were no spare dolls to entertain him, the man would simply go away and they could both continue playing as usual. She felt that once he had gone the world would return to the familiar one she understood.

However, Suzy – who was six months younger than Tina – was not as sophisticated in her thoughts; she simply wanted to help the stranger. She chewed on her bottom lip for a moment, and then smiled as she found a possible solution.

'I've got a box of other dolls in my yard at home. I just got them from my cousin Emma cos she's twelve and her mom thinks that's too old for dolls,' Suzy said. 'I could get one from there maybe – or I could get one from my room and you could play with that?'

Even then – without fully understanding why – Tina wanted to tell Suzy to shut up. She wanted to remind her that the stranger didn't belong in their game of Barbie dolls, plastic boats and toys in the dust, but it was too late.

'Wow,' the stranger's face lit up suddenly, 'that would be awesome. I mean I don't want you to go to any trouble just for me. No,' he shook his head emphatically, 'that would be too nice of you.'

'It's fine,' Suzy said as she got to her feet and dusted down her knees, 'I'll just be a minute.'

'You sure it's okay?' the stranger asked.

'Of course,' Suzy said, cheerfully, and then, whilst Tina looked around with a growing sense of confusion, her friend scrambled back up the crumbling track to the parking area. As she reached the top of the track, Suzy was so preoccupied with her task that she didn't notice something was different. There was now a dusty brown car sitting in a corner of the parking area that had not been parked there before.

When Suzy stepped out of her yard on to the dusty street, she felt the full heat of the afternoon sun. For a moment, she considered going back into the house to fetch her pink baseball cap, but it had already taken her fifteen minutes to rummage around for a discarded doll. Eventually, she found it lodged in the narrow space between her small mattress and her bedroom wall.

When Suzy returned, skipping carelessly through the needle grass, she arrived at the edge of the creek and stopped dead. A look of confusion crossed her sun-cream streaked face. There was no sign of either her friend or the stranger. Suzy brushed strands of hair from her small face and then frowned. She had not been away very long so she estimated that even if Tina and the stranger had moved around to play elsewhere, they should've been nearby.

After peering all around and swinging the doll by its golden hair, Suzy carefully descended the crumbling slope leading down to the dry stream.

'Tina!' she called, 'I'm back! I brought the extra doll for the man.' As she navigated the serpentine track, Suzy got no answer from the silent wilderness other than the creaky chirrup of crickets in the shadows of the sun-baked trees.

Yet the situation seemed impossible – there was nowhere that Tina and the stranger could have gone, so Suzy pushed on.

When she reached the exact place where they had been playing, Suzy discovered the two abandoned Barbie figures lying sprawled with their limbs at unnatural angles on the parched ground. The

Wet n Wild boat lay slightly further away as if it had been displaced by some freak wave. The entire scene looked like the sight of some recent miniature tragedy.

From somewhere nearby, Suzy could hear a regular and high-pitched sound. The small girl cocked her head and listened to the noise carefully. It was then, after a moment, that she recognised the noise; it was the distant sound of Tina's mother standing on the sun-bleached steps of her porch, calling on her only child.

1

The kid had to be dead, at least that was what Leighton Jones thought as he pulled up his black Explorer behind the mangled wreck of the red Fiat, which was sitting upside down on the edge of the Oceanside Highway.

Leighton suspected that few people could survive that level of impact, which had left the vehicle looking like a crushed soda can. The collision had apparently occurred less than thirty minutes earlier on a busy stretch of the hot highway, which ran along the southern side of the city. A shaken young trucker had called the accident in, stating that some young guy in front of him on the highway just had a blow-out, causing his car to skid sideways and flip like a scene out of a big budget action movie. Leighton and his partner – Teddy Leach – had arrived in a glossy black Ford Explorer which now sat an angle protecting the scene from further damage.

Racing out of the vehicle, Leighton waved the pale-faced trucker back from the debris, then dropped quickly into a crouching position amongst the diamonds of broken glass on the asphalt. The crunch of the fragments beneath his shoes sounded like tiny bones breaking. Whilst his partner quickly laid yellow cones in a wide barrier around the scene, Leighton peered into a triangular gap in the top of the mangled metal. He could see no obvious sign of life. However, there was an opening in the twisted wreckage lower down where it touched the tarmac. Leighton grunted as he shifted himself on to his belly, and then crawled towards the crushed opening.

'Shit,' he whispered. Glancing over his shoulder, he called to his partner. 'Teddy, tell dispatch to hurry that ambulance up!'

Returning his attention back to the wreck, Leighton could see the driver – a young man – tangled in the crushed remains of his car. He was lying curled in a foetal position on what had previously been the interior roof of the car. There were bloody stripes across the driver's face and the misshaped arm closest to Leighton looked as if it had probably snapped on impact. A green Magic Tree air-freshener was stuck to the kid's forehead, as if it was a strange fashion statement. Although the driver had been thrown out of the upside-down seat, he still had a seatbelt wrapped tightly around his lower body like a flat black snake.

Having spent ten years working in the traffic division of Oceanside P.D. Leighton knew from experience that he had to get the kid out of the wreckage quickly. The surface of the road was blistering hot, which meant that the gasoline seeping from the gas tank was already evaporating. Any spark might blow the whole thing up like a cherry bomb.

'Can you hear me, kid?' Leighton called to the young man.

For a moment there was nothing but the roar of the nearby traffic in the two lanes that were still operational.

'Can you hear me, in there?' he tried again.

In response to this second attempt, the passenger groaned and gradually opened his eyes for brief moment before slowly closing them again.

'I'm going to get you out of here, okay?' Leighton said assertively.

The young man's eyes did not open again.

Wriggling into the tight space was trickier than Leighton had expected. The cramped cavity stank of blood, engine coolant and urine. Grimacing, Leighton reached into a compartment on his belt and produced a folding knife. After squirming in alongside the unconscious driver, Leighton used the blade to cut the seatbelt, releasing the kid's lifeless legs.

'Okay, buddy,' Leighton said as he folded the knife away, 'I'm going to have to drag you out the car. Might hurt a little bit.'

Wriggling backwards out of the vehicle, Leighton reached forward and gripped the young man by his damp shoulders. He then began to pull. He had expected a scream of pain from the casualty as his broken arm brushed upon the twisted remains of his vehicle, but thankfully he remained unconscious throughout the manoeuvre Leighton groaned as he inched out of the wreck. The force of dragging the young man sent a burning pain along both of his arms, but there was little room – or time – to do anything else.

Thankfully, when he was about halfway clear, he felt somebody reach a hand in beside him and help with the pulling.

'That you, Teddy?' Leighton asked, breathlessly.

'Yep,' his partner – Ted Leach – replied. 'Dispatch just confirmed that the ambulance is five minutes from here. The tailback on the boulevard might delay them. Is he alive?'

'I think so,' Leighton said. 'Don't know for how much longer though.'

Both officers eventually worked the young man free from the vehicle and carried him carefully to the dusty roadside. Once he had laid the kid on a police blanket, Leighton knelt by the casualty and began checking for vital signs. In addition to the broken arm the driver had a dark purple bruise on the top of his head – probably from where it had collided with the shattered windshield. But more alarming to Leighton was the blood from somewhere on the driver's back, which was seeping into the blanket.

Leighton put his ear to the young man's mouth and waited for a moment. He then slid two fingers onto his neck and checked for a pulse.

'Shit!' he said and suddenly pinched the man's nose, tilted his chin and covered his mouth with his own. Leighton breathed into him, trying to ignore that the young man's lips felt cool. Leighton then sat up and locked his hands together. As he began chest compressions, he glanced over his shoulder to see his partner using pink spray paint to mark out the skid marks on the tarmac.

'Teddy!' he yelled, 'get back down here – he's fading away!'

Teddy ran to the scene and dropped to his knees. Both officers fell into a well-rehearsed rhythm as they attempted to keep the heart beating and lungs inflating.

After a few minutes of CPR, they stopped and Leighton checked again for a pulse. Teddy raised his eyebrows hopefully, but Leighton shook his head. Despite this, he was undeterred from his mission.

'Let's keep going,' he said.

'C'mon, Jonesy,' Teddy sighed, 'the guy's not coming back. Nobody could survive that crash.'

'That's not our call to make,' Leighton said while continuing with the cycle of chest compressions and breaths. Teddy stood up and shook his head.

Finally, as Leighton's shoulders were starting to ache, he heard the swelling sound of an ambulance whining increasingly closer to him. The sound was reassuring, but it didn't distract Leighton from his purpose; he continued pressing on the young man's chest, and eventually only stopped working on the kid when the paramedics knelt by his side and took over.

Getting slowly to his feet, Leighton stepped back away from the casualty. He was breathing heavily and sweat was trickling down the neck of his uniform. At that moment, his partner stepped over to him with a frown creasing his forehead.

'You do realise that didn't need to keep going so long?' Teddy asked.

'Yes I did,' Leighton said and wandered towards the police car to write down the details of the incident in his notebook.

'It probably didn't make any difference,' Teddy called weakly after him. When that didn't get a response he tried something stronger.

'We're meant to be a team; it's no wonder nobody wants to work with you!'

Leighton turned around and glanced across the hot roadside at the younger officer, who –with six months experience on the job – felt confident enough to call out a more experienced cop's decisions. At this stage in his career Leighton had fifteen years of experience on the roads of Oceanside, but he wasn't about to get into a public pissing contest with a rookie. However, he wasn't about to let the shiny little officer get the last word on whether or not anybody else has a right to life.

'Well maybe that's true, but I promised the kid that I'd get him to safety,' Leighton said, resolutely, 'I owed it to him to try to keep my word. I reckon his life was worth more than my need to end my shift on time.'

Teddy opened his mouth to say something more but by the time he had formulated a response, Leighton had already walked towards the car. A few feet away, the driver – now strapped to a gurney - was wheeled into the waiting ambulance.

2

Tina was lying trembling in the cramped darkness of her small, dark prison. The rough material upon which she lay smelled of oil and gasoline. It reminded her of the smell of the place where her mom had taken her car to have new tyres fitted. The surface felt coarse and painful against the exposed skin of her arms and legs. She tried repeatedly to shift away from the fabric, but there wasn't enough room and Tina end up scraping her knees. It was both dark and extremely hot in the confined space.

Before the stranger had put her into the trunk of the car, he had led her from the creek to his car. At the time, Tina had been sick with fear. But she had no choice. Once Suzy had gone off in search of a doll, the stranger had leaned close to her. His breath smelled like cheap hot dogs.

'Your momma's name is Angela Blanchette and you're Tina, right?' he asked in a conspiratorial whisper.

Tina had nodded but avoided the stranger's intense gaze.

'Good.' The stranger nodded. 'Well, Tina, there isn't an easy way to say this so I guess I'll just come right out with it – I've come here to help save you from some very bad people.' He had frowned earnestly and watched Tina's face closely 'your mom sent me to help you.'

Tina frowned and tried to make sense of what she heard. It didn't work.

'But she's back at my house,' Tina said. 'I saw her before I left for Suzy's yard.'

'That's right,' the stranger had said with a smile. 'She's home but the bad people are watching your house from nearby. That's why your mom asked me to lead you away from here. When I get you to safety, I have to call her. Then your mom will drive up to meet us.'

'She said that?' Tina asked with a hopeful tone. All she wanted was to be with her mom.

'Yes she did,' the stranger nodded, 'on my boy scouts honour. But we need to be quick.'

'But, I haven't seen any people.'

'You wouldn't have because these bad people are very clever. They've been watching you for a while now – hiding in the woods and driving slowly behind you as you skip home from school.'

'How do you know?' Tina asked.

'I like to stop bad people. I got close to one of them in a bar. He was drunk and told me their plan – about how they would steal you. So, I called round to your home and I told your mom. I wanted to warn her, you see. Hell, she wasn't sure at first but I explained that no locked door or window could keep these people out. I told her that they said you have a Toy Story poster in your bedroom and a fluffy crocodile on your pillow – that's right, isn't it?'

Tina nodded in horror.

'And he said that your mom has a painting of the moon on her bedroom wall. That's right, isn't it?'

Tina nodded. The story seemed true, but as she realised how helpless she was Tina started to cry and shake. This didn't seem to bother the stranger who said he would take Tina to a safe place where her mom would be waiting. The only problem was that these bad people were everywhere watching out for her – and that was why she had to hide in the trunk – where if she made any noise when the car slowed down, the bad people would find her and hurt her real bad.

But now as she lay curled in the darkness of the rumbling car, Tina Blanchette wasn't entirely sure that she actually believed the story the stranger had told her. Her mom had always told her that if they got separated in town, or if she ever needed help, she should find a police officer. It didn't seem likely, even to a seven year old, that her mom would arrange to meet in some far-away place or ask somebody to lock her in the trunk of a smelly old car. This moment of realisation that the stranger might not be trusted was when the first wave of fear washed over her like some dark tide. If the stranger wasn't really protecting her from bad people, and he had lied to her, that meant that he was a bad person – and he had trapped her in the trunk of his car.

3

As she gripped the ivory coloured handset Angela Blanchette felt reality rapidly sliding away from her. Her heart was beating so powerfully she could actually hear it pounding. Whilst the phone began its ringing, Angela pressed her forehead on the wall, closed her eyes and mouthed a silent prayer.

After calling on her daughter for five minutes without success, Angela had taken a leisurely walk down the hot street to see which garden she was currently playing in. Mostly, she like to hang out with Suzy Bucowiz – who she had been friends with since kindergarten – but if she wasn't around, Tina would sometimes play with Tommy Carlson who lived next door to her. Tommy wasn't much of a talker but he had a large trampoline and a modest swimming pool in his backyard. The latter was a source of excitement for Tina and anxiety for her mother. Although Tina was a strong little swimmer, her mother often worried that she would slip and fall on the tiled edge of the pool. In her cruel imagination, Angela could easily visualise her daughter running along the side of the pool edge then slipping, foot first as if on a banana peel, before slamming backwards onto the edge of the pool – head cracking like a ripe watermelon.

On her way to the Bucowiz's home, Angela saw Suzy scrambling up from the creek on the opposite side of the road. She was struggling to carry an assortment of dolls and toys. If Angela had been much closer she might have noticed that one of the Barbie dolls belonged to her own daughter.

'Hi, Suzy,' Angela called. 'Is Tina over there with you?'

'She was,' Suzy said with a puzzled expression, 'but she's gone away somewhere.'

'Where?'

'I don't know,' Suzy shrugged, and one of the dolls clattered to the dusty ground.

'Did you see her go?' Angela asked with a feeling akin to something uncomfortable uncoiling in her guts. It took all of her strength not to grab the girl and shake the answer from her.

Suzy shook her head, and then kicked absently at the hot ground.

'So did you maybe have a fight?'

'No, she was playing with the Barbie boat down in the creek,' Suzy said in a matter-of-fact way. She mistakenly thought her words would offer Tina's mom some comfort.

Angela Blanchette felt as if she had been slapped.

'In the creek?'

'Yeah,' Suzy said with a small shrug of her shoulders, 'I left her there when I came up here to fetch a doll from my yard.'

'Oh God!' Angela pushed by Suzy and ran across the baked surface of the road to the path leading down into the creek.

Having crossed the debris of the parking place, Angela half stumbled and half slid down the overgrown path to the place where a tiny stream had once ran.

'Tina!' she shrieked, but the there was no answer. She turned round and stared in all directions, hoping to see some flash of colour of her daughter moving playfully through the trees. There was nothing.

Scrambling back up the slope towards the road, Angela repeatedly shouted her daughter's name. The climb seemed endless as she negotiated the narrow dusty track. Eventually she emerged back at the roadside. Not far away, Jackie Bucowiz was coming out of her drive holding Suzy's hand.

'Hey, Angie, everything okay, honey?' she yelled across the road.

'I can't find her,' Angela said in a voice that was cracking. 'I can't find Tina!'

'Oh, shit,' Jackie seemed about to slide into panic, but somehow composed herself at the last minute. 'Right, get over here!' she called. 'Don't worry – we'll find her.'

Angela nodded and hurried across the road to where the woman and child were standing.

'Right,' Jackie crouched down to speak to her daughter face-to-face, 'honey, when did you last see Tina?'

'A little while ago,' Suzy said.

'Where was this?'

'At the creek.' Suzy shrugged her shoulders and began combing her fingers through her doll's hair.

'She's not there, I checked.' Angela glanced anxiously all around.

'Did you guys have a fight?'

'No.'

'So why did you come back to the house?'

'To get a doll, we needed an extra one.' Suzy's tone suggested it was an obvious situation and didn't require further explanation.

'Another doll? Why – you already had some?' Jackie asked.

'We needed one for the man, silly.' Suzy shrugged.

'What man?' Angela's head snapped around to stare at the girl.

'The one with the glasses, who was with Tina. He wanted to join in our game but he didn't have a doll. That's why I had to come up here to get one.'

'Oh, Jesus!' Angela said, as the gravity of the situation engulfed her. She turned and ran, her cheap sandals slapping loudly on the hot ground, towards her own home. As the sound of her own frantic breathing filled her head, she was oblivious to Jackie calling her name.

After clattering through the screen door of the house, Angela scrambled through the hallway to the telephone. It seemed almost too slippery to hold as she grabbed the glossy handset.

Now as she held the plastic telephone in one trembling hand, waiting for the sheriff's department to answer, Angela felt like the entire world was rapidly disintegrating around her.

When David had slipped into the grip of his mid-life crisis, leaving her and Tina in the wake of his departure to start his new life in Alaska, Angela had felt like it was the end of her happy ever after.

Now, two years later, Tina getting taken, felt like the end of everything.

4

Dressed in a checked gown over a white vest and shorts, Len Wells shuffled out on to the small porch of his home in the Sunbeam Garden Retirement Village and eased himself into the red and white striped beach chair. The neat little porch was overhung by a small tiled roof beneath which small birds and the occasional rock lizard would regularly take shelter from the Californian sun. Some people might have resented these small intruders, but with no family, friends or pets, Len appreciated the fleeting company.

Gripping the edge of the flimsy chair for support, Len adjusted his stained robe before attempting to sit. For him, sitting outside was a delicate process. Neither his own body nor the faded chair were as reliable as they had once been, and on at least one occasion he had found himself tumbling gracelessly to the ground. However, on this occasion the manoeuvre went smoothly.

Having settled into the chair, Len reached down for an ivory coloured cool box he kept on the deck. With a trembling hand, he pulled out a small fat glass and a bottle of amber coloured bourbon. Len unscrewed the cap then poured himself a glass, deliberately leaving the top off the bottle. He then made a silent toast to a small girl called Maria; she had been small for her age and had a bright smile that seemed to radiate happiness. Even all these years later, Len could not forget that infectious smile.

He raised the glass to his stubbled face, tipped it back and sipped the amber liquid. It tasted warm and sweet.

From some nearby road, the sound of a police siren rose, whooping towards a crescendo then falling away again. To Len Wells it sounded like and echo from his past. He smiled bitterly.

In response to the sound, the image of a second child rose in his mind, floating to the surface like a waxy balloon.

'I'm sorry,' Len mumbled. If the old man was aware of the tears sliding down his strained face, it didn't show. He simply picked up the glass again. This time he tipped it back and swallowed the entire contents.

Having emptied the glass, he set it down and poured out another one. Then he turned his left wrist, stared at the face of his watch. Three forty-five pm. He let out a silent sigh, then tipped the drink into the back of his throat.

5

The vehicle seemed to have been rumbling on forever. Every so often it would speed up for a while, then slow almost to a stop. The relentless rocking motion was making Tina feel increasingly sick. It reminded her of the time an accident on the highway meant her school bus needed to take a detour along some twisting back road. The twenty-minute experience had felt like it lasted for hours, and had left Tina feeling sick for most of that morning at school.

Suddenly the car slowed and lurched to a complete stop. The momentum threw Tina against the far end of the trunk. The engine sound fell suddenly silent. It was then that she heard the stranger rolling down his window. Tina held her breath as she heard his voice call to someone. The sound was muffled but still discernible.

'Get that goddamned thing out of the way,' the stranger called. 'You're blocking the goddamned road!'

In the absence of any visual, Tina's hearing had suddenly become the most important of all her senses. As she listened, she noticed that the stranger's voice sounded different from when he had spoken to her and Suzy back at the creek. Back then, he had sounded almost like a weird big kid, but now he just sounded like any other adult man.

'I can't. It's too heavy. You'll need to give me a hand – or we'll both be stuck,' a different voice replied. This was followed by some incoherent mumbling and then she heard the car door open and slam shut with a bang.

Tina waited for a tense moment, half expecting the trunk to open and the stranger to look down on her, but the trunk remained shut. Listening intently, Tina became aware of voices coming from somewhere nearby.

In the confusion of her confinement, Tina came to a clear realisation – she had to escape. This was not a normal rational thought, produced by a process of careful deliberation, but rather it came from some primitive self-preservation mechanism which had abruptly switched on like a shrieking alarm, telling her she was in real danger. Although she was only seven years old, Tina was an intelligent child who had come out of her parent's separation with a quiet gift for observation. She was aware that the world was capable of changing, that a trapdoor could open and she could fall into instant chaos. Tina's breathing quickened as adrenalin began to course through her tiny body. The only light in the airless space came in the form of a bright line where the lid of the trunk did not meet with the body of the car completely. Leaning on her side she pushed her face up to this gap. She squinted against the light, but was unable to see anything through the space. She tried pushing her fingertips into the gap but it was simply too small. Deciding to try a different approach, Tina rolled over on to her opposite side, and pushed her arms out in front of her. She was now facing the rear of the trunk. She remembered that in her mom's car part of the trunk opened like a small hatch leading into the back seat. She had seen it in action one day when her mom had bought a new curtain pole from some shop in Barstow. That day she had sat in the back of the car – she only ever sat in the back because her mom said that was safer – and she had watched in fascination as the curtain pole pushed from the trunk into the seat next to her. She was entranced by the idea of a secret doorway leading to another part of the vehicle. It was like a secret escape hatch.

Now, locked in the stranger's car, Tina hoped that it had a similar hatch. She tried not to panic as her small fingers carefully traced the shape of the material on the surface closest to her. Breathing quickly, she ran her hands back and forth on the scratchy surface until they found an area that was suddenly smooth and hard. Pushing her hand into this small indentation she realised that it felt like the handle on her mom's washing machine. Gripping the smooth plate was difficult with fingers that were slick with sweat. At first, they just slipped off, but she made a small fist and levered it against the handle. Closing her eyes, Tina ignored the pain, then heard an audible click. Suddenly the entire surface fell away from her. A blinding shaft of sunlight fell on Tina's face and she had to hold up her hand to shield her eyes. She discovered that rather than a hatch, she had actually opened the entire backrest of the rear seat of the car she had been locked in. The backrest was now leaning forward at a sharp angle.

Reaching into the bright interior of the car, Tina half crawled from the trunk on to the fuzzy material of the car seat. The brightness engulfing Tina was so strong that she had to keep her eyes almost closed. With her balled fists pressed into the material, and her sweaty hair tangled around her face, she looked like an alert lion cub as she gazed around. From this position she could peek between the twin headrests and observe the stranger through the windshield. At first, she didn't recognise him. His hair was short and cut close to his head with the exception of a dark lock falling across his forehead. Confused, Tina glanced down to the passenger seat where the discarded glasses lay beside the red baseball cap. She then looked back at the stranger and recognised the clothes. This was the same man. He was several yards ahead, helping an elderly man move a large metal trailer that seemed to have fallen off the other man's car. It was sitting almost sideways, half in the tall grass which grew on either side of the road. This made the stranger seem momentarily kind, and Tina felt that perhaps she should trust him. This feeling changed, however, when she glanced down again and noticed that the baseball cap had hair attached with silver coloured taped to its inside rim. He had been disguising himself.

In a moment of cool maturity, Tina glanced back up at the stranger and realised that this would probably be her only chance to return back home to her mom. Part of her wanted to cry, allowing hot tears to bubble down her face and wait for somebody to help – but the only adult who could help was her main threat.

She had to be brave, like the time she fell the previous summer whilst learning to riding her bike. The syrupy blood had run down her leg and stained her white shoes, but she cycled home regardless and her mom had patched her up.

Crawling carefully through the wedge-shaped opening, Tina panicked, thinking that she somehow would become stuck and the stranger would come back to find her trapped, caught in the act of trying to escape. Thankfully, her skinny body slipped through the space without much of a struggle.

Once she had wriggled free of the back seat, Tina pushed it closed and reached her small hand for the door handle on the side furthest from where the stranger was. All the while she kept her small eyes fixed on the stranger. Luckily, he was facing away from her as he struggled with the other man to move the obstacle.

The door clicked softly as Tina opened it and quietly slipped out of the passenger side of the car. The body of the vehicle remained between her and the stranger, as Tina gently closed the door behind her and then crawled on all fours like a kitten into the long grass.

As soon as she was clear of the car and hidden among the taller bushes, Tina got to her feet and ran as fast as she could. Her feet slapped off the dusty ground as some primitive survival instinct sent her thundering forward. She brushed the tall dried plants aside as she rushed through the brittle undergrowth. With little sense of where she was going, Tina hurtled deeper into the wilderness. Even when a dull pain in her side began to form, she kept moving, all the time aware that in the fields behind her, the stranger was looking for her.

6

Leighton was half listening to the *Coping with Loss* cassette whilst driving home from work along a dusty Olive Hill Road on the north side of the city. Oceanside was an area characterised by rust coloured hills and parched planes of land studded with the sturdy cacti which sat among an infinite carpet of needle grass.

Today, like most days in California, was hot, and despite the mellow tone of the cassette, Leighton found it more irritating than relaxing. The disclaimer at the start of the recording gravely stated that it should not be listened to *whilst driving or operating machinery*. He had smiled at this advice – as far as he was concerned they were both the same thing. In the previous ten years, he had often seen just how dangerous three tons of hot metal moving at forty mph could be.

Glancing at his hand gripping the wheel, Leighton noticed that it was still stained from the earlier incident. A streak of blood from the young driver had dried to rusty crumbs on the back of his fingers. Leighton sighed. He knew Teddy would probably report him for not wearing the standard issue latex gloves whilst administering medical treatment to a member of the public. Any such report would be nothing new either. In the six months they had been working together, Teddy had reported him on six separate occasions. Prior to working with the rookie, Leighton had never been summoned by the captain. It was therefore obvious that every lapse in protocol was being recorded and reported. On the first occasion, Teddy had gone directly to Chief Winston and complained that Leighton was too lax with completing paperwork. Thankfully, the chief had bigger things to worry about than admin and had suggested that perhaps Teddy should probably concentrate on developing his own skills rather than identifying flaws in more experienced officers. However, privately he had summoned Leighton to his office and advised him to be more careful around his new partner.

Although Leighton had not confirmed it, he suspected that this eagerness to report colleagues had been the reason for Teddy's previous two-month partnership with another officer – Danny Clarke – falling apart. Danny, who was a few years younger than Leighton, was known to be a decent cop. Leighton figured if things had not worked out with the two of them, it had most probably been the rookie's problem rather than Danny's.

Even without Teddy's unwelcomed scrutiny, it had already been a tricky afternoon. Leighton was confident that Teddy would undoubtedly snitch on him for spending too much time trying to keep the kid alive today, but Leighton didn't care.

This time they would most likely blame his actions on grief, and then find some bullshit way of linking it back to Heather's death. It wasn't true; Leighton would have tried to save the young guy whether or not his wife had still been alive. In any case, at least he was trying to play the game in terms of his emotional well-being.

The hypnosis tape, a gift from his grief counsellor – James Hernandez, was designed to help alleviate Leighton's stress at the end of each day. As he had sat self-consciously in the therapist's office, Hernandez had told him that it was necessary to reduce the stress in his life in order to allow natural grieving to occur. As far as Leighton was concerned there was nothing natural about grieving. To him it seemed as if a bomb had exploded in the middle of his life and now he had to carry on living in a world of splinters and ash, acting like everything was normal. However, he was willing to jump through whatever hoops might possibly allow him to get back to some sort of normality. For Leighton, normality meant being able to function as cop, but more importantly as a father to Annie.

So he reluctantly accepted the cassette tape and agreed to listen to the soothing melodies and comforting affirmations on a regular basis. The problem was that he couldn't sit at his desk and play it in the station whilst surrounded by thirty-five other cops; Leighton figured that some of them were too relaxed already. Neither did he want to play the therapy tape after he had picked up his daughter Annie from the child-minder at the end of each day. That time was their only opportunity to relax together and make up for lost time.

But despite this, Leighton accepted that he should at least become familiar with the content just in case the therapist asked him about it in their weekly meetings. Although it had never been explicitly said aloud, it was apparent that Leighton's continuing role serving with Oceanside P.D. was dependent on him being given a clean bill of psychological health. If part of getting through the game required him listening to the required self-help tape then Leighton was willing to give a shot – just not publicly.

Therefore, listening to the cassette during the journey home seemed like a good option; no distractions, no audience. He slotted the cassette into the mouth of the player and then took a few deep breaths. Leighton wasn't convinced that the mellow sound of the recording helped fill the dark chasm inside him. It didn't seem sufficient enough to lighten the weight of imminent mortality baring down upon him, but at least taking some type of positive action might just help keep him breathing a little while longer.

7

His instincts had told him something was wrong. He had felt like a disturbance somewhere deep in his mind, and he should have listened to it. It was always the same – starting with a strange fizzing sensation in his skin, building up to a full-on trembling sensation in both arms. It was the closest thing he knew to fear, and it had happened once before, back in the scorching summer of 1986.

That had been the summer when his dark urges had first become impossible to resist. They had been simmering for a couple of years prior to that, but in that particular season, his need to take a child had been so powerful it had been inescapable. Despite his skill in snatching the kid from the play park, he had seriously messed up. It was a dumb error, and part of his learning curve. He had simply left the stolen kid in the trunk for too long in an exposed parking area of the national park. At the time, he had driven out of the city to the remote area. At one point he had considered stopping at a mall parking lot, but he knew that those places increasingly seemed to have cameras everywhere. Escaping into the wilder places seemed liked a better option. But it had been a hot day and as he had sat in slow lanes of traffic, Leighton knew that he should check that the recently acquired kid was alive. The journey out of the city had taken him into the desert heat of the highway, which ran north-east towards Fallbrook. Eventually, he found a parking area at the start of the Guajome Regional Park. However, just as the stranger pulled and switched off the engine, a couple of park rangers pulled in alongside him. By that time, descriptions of the missing kid had been all over the radio. It would have looked too weird for him to have sat in the car while two rangers enjoyed their lunch, so he got out of the car and wandered off. He got into his head the rangers might hear some noise coming from the car and investigate it. In order to get himself out of harm's way, he drifted steadily out on the baking road and hitched a ride from a bearded truck driver back into the city.

He had returned to his trailer and taken a cool bottle of beer from the refrigerator. Slumping on the battered couch, he twisted the cap off the bottle and then tossed it into the corner of the room. He felt like a starving creature who had been given a delicious meal, only to have it ripped away from him before he could take a bite. Cocking his head to one side, he listened to the distant moan of a police siren. As it faded into silence, he tilted the bottles and gulped it down in a private celebration of his continuing liberation.

His mind shifted from the risk of getting caught to the passenger hidden in the darkness of the trunk. It looked like he would be spending the night there. And deserts could get a bit chilly too. Still, he figured that the kid would most likely be alright. No car trunk was ever airtight, so he would be able to breath, plus there was an old tarpaulin in there too. The kid could use that if he got cold.

Given that everything seemed cool, he got up and walked back to the refrigerator. Took out another beer. He held the door open allowing the cold air to cool his sweating face. The stranger thought for a moment about whether or not he should have a second beer, but he figured that he wouldn't be going anywhere soon. After a moment of further considerations, he reached back in and removed the rest of the six-pack.

He took the beers outside, to where a tattered folding chair sat next to his trailer on the western edge of the Sun View caravan park.

Easing himself into the chair he opened his beer and began drinking. His chair was strategically located, although it was tilted towards his own trailer. He had attached an old cracked shaving mirror to the outside wall of his unit. This meant he could relax any evening and watch the kids who lived on the park – scooting about on their bikes or chasing each other around – without arousing suspicion. On hot nights they would be wearing less. He liked that.

Eventually, his thoughts of the kid locked in the trunk of his car – and the associated fears of getting caught – were eclipsed by the cold alcohol running through his bloodstream, as well as the inevitable craving for more. Stepping back up inside the trailer, he rummaged through the debris of his lair until he found a half empty bottle of bourbon beneath a cluttered coffee table. He dragged it out and unscrewed the cap off the bottle. Tilting his head back, he brought the bottle to his cracked lips and drank the darkness.

***

By the time he had taken a stuffy taxi cab ride back to the location at the edge of the sprawling national park, twenty-four anxious hours had passed. But the stranger had not arrived without provisions. He had brought a plastic bottle of water and a packet of cookies, to help revive the kid. Having paid the taxi driver a bundle of crumpled twenties, he stood back and waited for him to leave the remote parking spot. Once the cab had trundled away in a cloud of hot dust, the stranger finally hurried over to the car and opened the trunk. Even then, in the act of opening that lid, he noticed that the metal of the car felt almost too hot to touch. It was then he discovered that the baking heat of exposed car had been too much for his passenger. After closing the trunk then sitting in the dust where he ate most of the cookies, he had driven the car for almost an hour, before dumping the wasted remains in a dusty ravine.

But that had been an error.

This time, however, he had been determined not to make the same mistake.

***

By the time he had finally dragged the old idiot's trailer to the side of the road, an impatient tailback of six honking cars had formed behind his own one. Despite a gnawing urge to check on his passenger, he knew he couldn't risk opening the trunk. Instead, he had jumped back in his car and driven a mile or so away until he found a quiet stretch of road. After checking his mirror, he slowly pulled over on the verge. He switched off the engine, and checked the road once again. It was still empty. He then reached beneath the driver's wheel, pulled a lever to unlock the trunk and hurried out of the car.

However, this time when he peered into the dark cavity the body was gone.

The empty trunk still smelled of the absent child, and the sense of his loss caused him something akin to pain and rage. He knew even before he leaned in to the humid cavity, and pushed the unsecured backrest forwards that this was how she had escaped. The growl of pain and which escaped from his mouth sounded completely guttural.

Slamming the lid of the trunk shut, he climbed back into the car and revved away in a cloud of dust. The kid had seen his face – she knew what the car looked like too. Even if he hadn't been consumed by the thrill of ending her life, there was no way he was going to let the little bitch get away.

8

'Oceanside Police, how may I help?' The voice on the telephone sounded cool and efficient.

'My daughter is missing.' Angela gulped the words out, the phrase seeming to stick in her throat. 'Please, you have to find her.'

'What's your name, please?' The voice sounded unfazed by Angela's words.

'Please,' Angela said, as she ran a hand through her sweat-dampened hair, 'you've got to help me!'

'I hear you, ma'am, we just need some details from you, and then we can help. Can you give me your full name?'

'Angela Blanchette.'

'Any middle names?'

'No.'

'And your address, Mrs Blanchette?'

'Four hundred and seven Alta Vista Drive, Fallbrook.'

'Is this your home number that you're currently calling from?'

'Yes,' Angela said, 'Jesus, yes!'

'Can I have your daughter's full name?'

'Christina Blanchette – but we call her Tina.'

'Thank you. When did you last see Tina?'

'Around 2.00 – maybe 2.30 this afternoon.'

'Can you confirm your daughter's date of birth?'

Angela had to fight the urge to pass out as she recalled Tina's birthday. 'It's ten, eighteen, ninety.'

'So she's seven years old, is that correct?'

'Yes.'

'Hair colour?'

'Light brown. Is all of this goddam necessary – she's missing!' Angela blurted. 'My daughter is missing!'

'I understand, Mrs Blanchette, these details will help us find your daughter. Now where did you last see Tina?'

'She was here in the house about an hour or so ago. She left our house to go play with her friend who lives nearby. But her friend says a man came along and spoke with them, and now she's missing.'

'Okay, Mrs Blanchette, somebody will be with you soon. Please, be aware that we receive many missing person's reports every week, and almost all of them are nothing to worry about.'

'Please hurry,' Angela said in a quiet and desperate voice.

After she put the phone down, she paced the length of her small home. She rubbed her hands restlessly together as she moved. Her mind kept turning over and over as if there was some solution, some logical explanation she was somehow missing. Perhaps there was some arrangement she'd forgotten about, or perhaps Tina had fallen asleep in the woods. But none of that was the reality. Tina had been taken by some sick bastard. And Angela knew it too. She knew the man had taken her. There was no other logical explanation for her disappearance. Angela rushed into the bathroom and threw up in the toilet.

9

Tina was crouched like some wild creature on the hot dust in the middle of a patch of wilderness. The yellow grass around her was tall and thin but not particularly dense. It reminded Tina of the strands of dried spaghetti she had once used in kindergarten to make a picture of a scarecrow for her mom. At the time she had enjoyed sticking the brittle pieces all over the paper, but Tina had been unsettled by the grinning face with a lurid carrot for a nose. After her mom had proudly stuck the picture on to the side of the refrigerator at home, Tina had snuck in, taken down her creation, before scrunching it up and dropping it in the trash can.

In the ten minutes since her escape from the stranger, Tina had stopped only momentarily to regain her breath, but it was at those few seconds of rest that the tears finally came, drenching her small cheeks in a sudden deluge. Her head hung downwards and her tears dripped from her chin on to the parched ground. She wiped at her face, streaking it with the dust from her fingers.

The upset was only natural. In a period of a couple of hours, her entire world view had suddenly shifted from the predictable geography of her relatively stable little world of school and home to an unfamiliar chaos of infinite dangers and frightening landscapes. She knew now that she and Suzy should never have gone to the creek alone. It had been stupid and her mom would be angry with her. But Tina knew that she would be safe with an angry mom, and that was what she wanted most of all.

Eventually, when the tears had subsided, she wiped at her eyes and cheeks, then looked up. It was then in the stillness of her gesture that she heard the stranger call out to her from across the countryside. The sound chilled her blood. The call sounded like that of a blind and hungry ogre from some dark fairy tale. In the silence that followed, Tina stayed frozen in position. The rapid rise and fall of her chest was the only sign she was alive. In her mind, she could easily imagine the stranger creeping through the fields scanning from side to side. The image was horrific enough to break her paralysis. Getting cautiously to her feet, Tina glanced around trying to locate which direction the yelling was coming from. At first the sound was indistinct and difficult to locate, but then when she tilted her head and listened carefully, Tina could locate it.

The voice was not close, but it was growing in volume. Turning away from the sound, Tina ran as fast as she could in the opposite direction. She no longer cared what she was running towards as long as she was getting further and further away from the calls.

10

As he drove along the twisting road of Old Mill Way in his old Nissan, Leighton was lost in thought. The earlier heat of the afternoon was finally beginning to ebb and the groaning air conditioner no longer had to struggle to keep the car cool. Leighton had deliberately chosen to slip off the busier road home and meander out to the north-east fringes of the city where buildings were sparse and the roadside was often fringed by misshapen cacti and sun-bleached trees. In some areas, patches of wild grasses grew like forests of golden spears. This route offered a substantial contrast to the packed highways which locked up the city roads at key times of the day. This was because quite often some minor collision would mean that the sluggish traffic would eventually grind to a frustrated halt, leaving officers like Leighton and his colleagues to sort out the chaos.

Thankfully, this was a more relaxed journey for Leighton, one in which he would be given some privacy. Out here he didn't need to control his thoughts or appear to be coping.

Whilst the relaxed voice wafting through the stereo droned on about deep breaths and melting muscles, he was lost in a fog of thought. He was thinking about Annie and wondering how he could possibly make things better for her, though perhaps he never could. A child needed a mother – especially a little girl. How could an unstable cop dad possibly fill the gap? There was little chance of him finding a partner again. Not after how badly he let Heather down.

***

At the start, before the dark days consumed Heather entirely, things had been good – at least he thought they had. For a couple of years, Leighton and Heather had simply been a young couple lost in the bliss of possibility. In his fading memories those lost days had been warm, and their shared future had seemed filled with possibilities. He had been a rookie cop and she had been taking a correspondence class to teach kindergarten. Throughout those youthful seasons, they had spent countless afternoons at the harbour and beach, often sharing a towel and enjoying the soft proximity of each other. But even then, there had been occasional moments when Heather would grew quiet and distant. She would stare at the ocean, mute and unreachable. If Leighton tried to get her to speak about it, Heather would talk vaguely of sometimes feeling trapped in her own life. Leighton – who was happy with their life – could not understand.

Then, when Annie had eventually been born, things had begun to change much more dramatically. It wasn't a gradual slide, but rather a sudden shift from light to dark. He had watched the light go out in Heather's eyes. In a matter of months life became an unbearable burden for Heather, who retreated increasingly into herself until – eventually – she vanished entirely. Leighton had wanted desperately to help Heather, but it had felt like he was often reaching into an abyss. He had taken a six-month leave of absence to raise Annie and try to help Heather, but in the end she had spent every day in bed sleeping or facing the wall. The silence between them grew and eventually turned to resentment.

Over the next five years, Heather found the presence of her husband to be an endless irritation, his constant attempts to soothe her were an unwelcome intrusion. Leighton, without any other coping strategies, busied himself entirely with his daughter and his work. He knew even then that it wasn't the right approach, but then he wasn't sure what the right approach would be.

When Heather could no longer bear sharing her bleak home with her husband, she booked a yellow cab and moved out into her elderly parents' home. It was a three-and-a-half-hour drive away. Leighton – struggling to raise a five-year-old, had hoped she was doing this to give herself breathing space to get better.

He had been wrong. Three months after moving into the house on Primrose Avenue, Heather – who refused to answer any calls or come out of her room when Leighton brought Annie to visit – took a fatal dose of sleeping pills. There was no suicide note or explanation.

The loss had broken him; as a man and a husband he had failed. His wife had drifted out of existence, and he felt that he had allowed it to happen. This left his daughter without a mother, and stuck with a dysfunctional father.

And yet this single fact – his sole responsibility – made it necessary for him to somehow make things okay for Annie. If it had been his fault that things were bad, it was also his duty to put things right. That was his only means of redemption.

Now, in the absence of anyone else to share the roles, Leighton stared through his windshield and figured he would have to commit to learning how to braid hair and paint nails, and make it through.

It was then, when Leighton was caught up in his critique of his inadequate parenting that it happened.

The figure of what appeared to be a child, if that was what the apparition was, burst suddenly out of the tall grass at the side of the road and ran blindly across the road in front of his car.

In that instant, Leighton saw nothing more than a momentary orange blur in the shape of a child – there for a moment, then gone. In instinctive response, he slammed on the brakes of his car. It skidded to a squealing halt on the hot road surface. The momentum threw him forward, his seatbelt digging painfully into one shoulder. Leighton let out a deep sigh, and his hands, still fastened on the wheel, began to tremble.

'Jesus,' he muttered.

Having managed to coax one hand off the wheel, Leighton switched on his hazard lights, and unclipped his seatbelt. He then opened the door and climbed out into the warm evening air. The road and the surrounding area were so quiet he could hear the faint hushing sound of the restless surf, punctuated by the chirrup of bugs in the grass. Wandering around the car, Leighton peered into the long grass, door handle-high, at the side of his car. It had been less than a minute since the child had slipped into the grass, yet the area appeared undisturbed. Leighton took a cautious step into the dusty wilderness and called out across the parched landscape.

'Hey, kid, are you okay? Is someone with you?' Leighton's deep voice carried on the warm evening air.

He waited for a moment, standing on the road, listening intently and staring out into the panorama of grass and trees stretching toward the rocky distant hills.

'Can you hear me, kid?' he yelled, and held his hand up to shield his eyes from the low afternoon sun.

There was no answer other than the slow ripple of the needle grass and the relentless creak and whirr of the hidden oblivious insects.

Staring into the wilderness, Leighton wondered for a moment if he had somehow imagined the child. Perhaps she was something his mind had conjured up from a mixture of tiredness and a relaxation cassette. He knew from experience that a tried mind could create all sorts of images. He had once pulled a guy from a near fatal car wreck, who had swerved off the road to avoid a white tiger in the middle of the road. Two other eye-witnesses had confirmed that the road had been entirely empty, and the driver confessed that he had been driving with almost no sleep for two days – attempting to drive non-stop from Mexico to Portland for a family wedding. Despite this clear explanation for the hallucination, the driver still insisted that the white tiger had been real.

Leighton knew that the mind could do some strange things, but in this instance Leighton wasn't entirely convinced that his girl had been imaginary. Even in the minutes after she had gone, he could still see the shape of her in shorts and T-shirt, vanishing into the grass. The image of this small figure seemed to remain locked in his mind like a small ghost. It was simply as if she had been there for a moment, then vanished.

Eventually, a bird screeched somewhere in the sky above Leighton, pulling him from his confused thoughts. He turned from the deserted location and climbed back into his car. Whatever the story was with the kid, it didn't look like she was coming back. Leighton figured she was probably some local girl involved in a game with a bunch of other kids who would soon be roaming the area trying to find her. In any case, he had his own little girl at home to think of.

Reaching down to the jangling bunch of keys, Leighton started the engine, pushed the stick to drive and moved away from Old Mill Way.

11

The stranger on the opposite side of the road had been so caught up in his pursuit of the child that he almost blindly followed her out of the scrubland and straight into the path of the cop. This had been a situation he had never had to manage before – none of the others had ever escaped, and so he was functioning entirely on a combination of panic, rage and desperation. Luckily, the vehicle abandoned in the middle of the road was bright red – glaring through the yellow grass like an oversized Coke can – otherwise he might never have noticed it. If he had raced out of his hiding place, he would surely have risked being caught. There was nothing to explain stumbling out of the grass moments after the girl. Instead, the stranger – who had been close to catching up with the girl as she hurried towards the road – had instinctively stopped when he heard the sudden squeal of skidding tyres.

At first, he had suspected that the car had hit her. That would, of course, be the worst of all outcomes. All his effort and planning would be wasted if the girl simply ended up dead at the hands of somebody else – somebody who wouldn't actually savour the experience like he would.

However, if she was smeared into a bloody streak on the hot road, it would at least mean that the girl would no longer pose any risk to him. There was of course a more problematic possibility. The car may have hit the girl, but not killed her. If that was true then she would be able to describe his real appearance and his car… It was therefore important that he find out exactly what the situation was, before he decided on a course of action.

***

When the stranger realized that the car had stopped, he slunk instinctively back from the roadside and crouched down amongst the clumps of concealing grass. This position afforded him a view of the road, without the risk of being seen by the driver.

For a moment, the stranger considered retreating entirely, creeping backwards through the grass, but then he realized that the cop wasn't actually moving. He had his back to the stranger and was looking out into the field in the direction the girl had run. The fact the cop was looking away from the stranger was a bonus, but that didn't mean he wasn't about to turn around, and if he did that he would be looking directly at him.

The stranger let out his breath steadily and quietly. Blocked from crossing by the cop, he gradually lowered himself forward to his knees, placed his hand on the dusty ground and then lay down on his belly. Breathing silently like some hideous reptile, he watched the cop from between the brittle stalks. At that point, his attempt to remain invisible was still not required; the cop was just standing with his back to the stranger peering into the countryside on the opposite side of the road. For one moment, he had thought the cop would turn around and look in the stranger's direction, but he didn't. Instead he just continued peering out in the wilderness. Perhaps he hadn't actually seen the kid – that would explain his behaviour.

Eventually, the cop climbed back into the car and drove off. The stranger did not get up straight away. Instead he remained lying on his belly in the dust, breathing and watching. He knew how to be patient. In many ways, through all the years and all of his crimes, he enjoyed the waiting more than the action. It was the delicious excitement of possibility. This was simply a resting moment. With every passing second, he knew that the kid was getting further away, but he also knew that eventually she would grow tired, and he would outrun her.

Once the cop had driven away, the stranger remained lying on his chest in the dust for several minutes. He liked this proximity to the ground, the sensation of the heat of the earth warming his chest. It felt as if he belonged down there more than in the awkward upright world, with its quivering morality and fragile laws. The creatures that crawled and wriggled through the dusty ground could live as they pleased, take what they wanted without fear of judgment or punishment. He didn't understand why humans had to impose rules for themselves that went against the natural world. As far as he was concerned, life on earth involved billions of creatures attacking and killing every second of the day for all of history. It was natural. It was normal. And he was part of it.

Once he was confident that the cop wasn't going to be coming back, the stranger grunted and slowly got back to his feet. He then stepped silently out of the grass on to the warm road. He looked both ways and then, once he was satisfied that no other cars were around, he stared deep into the golden grass on the opposite side of the road. After gazing into the shifting blades for a moment, he licked his lips and ran suddenly forward into the wilderness. Within a few moments, the stranger had vanished into the hot landscape.

12

Breathing heavily, Tina stopped, turned around and looked uncertainly back in the vague direction of the road she had just crossed. Her desperation had kept forcing her onwards without any real sense of direction or purpose. At one point she had sensed that somebody was behind her – not necessarily close enough to hear properly, but the occasional crack of dried twigs seemed increasingly with regularity, forcing Tina to run onward again. This time, however, the journey had been harder. Her legs felt weak and her mouth was dry. Each step forward felt like it drained more of her energy. Yet, she had no choice, unless she was willing to go back inside the stifling trunk of the stranger's car. So she ran.

She had barely noticed the road until it was too late. Unable to stop, she had simply hurtled blindly forwards, propelled like a tumbling rock rolling downhill. And, as she burst out of the corn, the red car had almost hit her, she was sure of that. Despite the shock of that momentary brush with death, it still had not been enough to slow her down. She had continued running deep into the rough terrain until she was eventually swallowed by the landscape. Now she had stopped, Tina found herself surrounded by dry looking bushes and tufts of tall grass on all sides. From somewhere not too far behind, Tina heard the sound of a car door slam shut, like a gunshot, then a male voice called towards her.

'Hey, kid, are you okay? Is someone with you?'

The man's voice was not the same as the stranger's. He sounded different, normal – as if he might even help. In that moment, part of her desperately wanted to hurry through the dust to that comforting voice. The problem had been that she had run too well. If she had been even a few feet closer to the roadside, Tina would have been able to see that the man calling to her was actually wearing a black police uniform. Perhaps then she would have found the confidence to call back to him. But instead, Tina was too far away to see anything through the long grass. She also remembered how the stranger had been able to change his voice when he needed to. This realization made her turn away from the direction of the car and the man, and suddenly run deeper into the unfamiliar landscape. Her fear propelled her forwards, travelling further away from civilization. Rather than running towards some actual destination, Tina simply ran instinctively to escape from the threat.

Minutes later, Tina fell; tumbling painfully on to the dusty ground. Dried cactus needles stuck into her hands and knees and peppered her grazed skin. Unable to fight the inevitable tears that followed, Tina scrambled to her feet and continued running, her vision blurred, her limbs stinging. The combination of tears and exertion made breathing difficult.

All she wanted was to be held in her mom's soothing embrace, but she knew that was not going to happen unless she kept going. Pushing herself onwards, she ran and ran until she had no energy left and her sides were aching. Her hair hung around her face in sweaty strands, smearing the dust on her cheeks into dark streaks. By then she was too tired to even look around, and so she was initially unaware of the fact that the terrain around her had changed from flat grasslands to long sloping hills that stretched the length of the horizon. Tina knew that she had to find somebody to help her, and that climbing high up on to the slope would increase the chance of seeing somebody. Perhaps from that vantage point she might even see a house, or – even better – a familiar person. She knew that Suzy's dad often went hiking and mountain biking at the weekends, so, Tina thought she might even meet him.

So, with bleeding knees and craving fluids, the small girl in the orange T-shirt began wandering on to the sloping hills on the north-east side of Oceanside. By that point in her journey she was six miles away from the nearest house, and moving further away from it with every small step.

13

By the time he pulled up his car into the child-minder's drive, Leighton had almost forgotten about the kid on the road entirely. Instead, he was concerned about the smear of dried blood on his hand. After switching off the engine, he leaned across the passenger seat to the glove box and removed a packet of Wet Ones. He pulled a couple of tissues from the pack, and cleaned his hands. Before he had finished, the door of the house opened and Annie appeared. She was smiling and waving. Annie was clearly eager to get out of the doorway, but Maria Carrera was stuffing something into the back of her backpack. Leighton returned the infectious smile, and climbed out of the car.

'Hey, baby,' he said to Annie as the child-minder helped her down the steps. When she reached the bottom, Annie raced to Leighton who scooped her up and kissed her soft face.

'Hi, Daddy!' she said and then frowned at the scrape on his forehead. 'You got hurt.'

'It's okay, pumpkin – it's just a little scratch,' he said.

'Does it hurt?'

'No, baby. Your daddy's made of tough stuff.'

Annie traced a small finger over around the edges of the injury. 'I don't want you to be hurt,' she said.

'I know,' Leighton said and kissed her forehead. 'But I'm okay. Now let's get you into the car.'

As he opened the rear door, and Annie clambered into her rainbow patterned booster seat, Leighton turned his attention to the child-minder.

'Hi, Maria. Sorry I'm late. I hope she wasn't acting up.'

'It's fine. She's had a good afternoon,' Maria said. 'I think last week was just a blip. She just got herself worked up. Kids go through all sorts of worries, but most of them pass – it's just part of growing up.'

'I hope so,' Leighton said with a nervous smile. 'Thanks – Maria. I'll see you tomorrow.'

***

As they drove along the bustling highway towards the supermarket, Leighton enjoyed listening to his daughter chatting incessantly about her day. She was recounting a story about how her school buddy – Dale – had brought a clear glass marble in his lunch box, but their teacher – Mrs Goudy – had taken it off him in case anybody put it in their mouth.

'That's just silly,' Annie giggled at the idea, 'nobody eats marbles.'

'Well, sometimes people do silly things.' Leighton said. 'I think Mrs Goudy did the right thing.'

'But it was Dale's marble!' Annie's eyes widened in horror at the injustice.

'I know, baby, but Mrs Goudy probably gave it back to Dale's mom at the end of the day.'

This explanation seemed to satisfy Annie's sense of injustice – at least temporarily and she got distracted by passing vehicles. At one point she gazed to the distant northern horizon.

'Daddy, is that a storm heading our way?'

'Where?' Leighton peered in the rear-view mirror, trying to figure out where his daughter was looking.

'In the sky, those clouds.' Annie pointed her arm.

Following Annie's finger, Leighton looked towards the northern corner of the blue sky where three huge columns of grey smoke stretched into the air like slowly turning tornadoes.

'Don't worry; it's not a storm, baby,' Leighton said in a reassuring voice.

Annie bit her bottom lip and continued to gaze at the sky.

'What is it?' she asked.

'Smoke,' Leighton said, 'most likely coming off wild fires up on the hills.

'Who starts them – bad people?'

Leighton chuckled. 'No, honey – not usually. It just gets awful hot up there under the sun, and there are dried old trees everywhere. Sometimes when the sun shines through an old piece of glass it makes the wood so hot that it catches fire, and then it just spreads from bush to bush and tree to tree.'

'Wow,' Annie's eyes widened. 'That's real bad, right?'

Leighton realized that this could rapidly develop into one of her many current anxieties, so he thought it best to offer some reassurance.

'Yeah, I guess, but we live down near the ocean, and there's plenty of water there, right?'

'Good,' Annie said, 'I hate fires.'

**

It wasn't until he pulled his car into the busy parking lot of the Viva Market that Leighton realized how late it was – almost a quarter after six. That meant he had been almost an hour late picking up Annie. Dinner would have to be a quick and simple option. Annie would be both tired and hungry, which combined could make for an emotional evening.

'What do you fancy for supper, kiddo?'

'Anything,' Annie said.

'Well, how about we grab something to eat here?' he suggested.

'Like what?'

Leighton pulled a masterstroke. 'How about pizza?'

'Yay, pizza!' Annie jumped up and down in her booster seat.

**

Leighton smiled as he watched his daughter gleefully devour triangles of margarita. He occasionally sipped his coffee and gazed around at the assortment of diners. They all appeared to be young families, busily sharing food and laughing together. Happy.

When they had finished eating, Leighton and Annie picked up some groceries – essentials mainly, but Annie had also picked up a brightly collared book of fairy tales. She was an avid reader and Leighton wanted to encourage it as much as possible. Annie had asked if she could carry the book to the car, but Leighton refused, knowing that she would be unable to resist looking at it. He was trying to teach her road sense, and parking lots could be dangerous places – especially for distracted seven-year-olds.

Once they had returned to the car, Leighton put the keys in the ignition and made an almost subconscious decision. Instead of simply driving out of the parking lot and following his normal route home to carry on with his typical day, he retraced his earlier route back to Old Mill Way.

Pulling up at the edge of the road, he switched off the engine. It seemed like only a moment since Leighton had last been there.

'Where are we?' Annie asked as she glanced around at the dusty landscape.

'Just at a section of road I wanted to see.'

'For work?' she asked.

'Yeah,' Leighton nodded, 'for work. Clever girl.'

'Okay,' Annie shrugged happily. 'Can I have my book please?'

'Sure.' Leighton reached into the grocery bag on the passenger seat, found the book and passed it back to his daughter.

While Annie became lost in turning the pages of fairy tales, Leighton got out of the car.

Old Mill Way was a quiet road, which snaked along the northeast side of the city. This was the point at which the city faded into wilderness. The occasional private housing developments, which were dotted around the fringes of the city didn't quite extend this far. The irregular landscape, which was scarred with gullies and creeks would cost too much to flatten.

The natural chaos wasn't just limited to the landscape. The road Leighton's car was parked on was an old farm road and would require major upgrading for a couple of miles if it was ever going to carry more than a dozen or so cars each day. The combination of poor quality roads and the arid landscape meant there was nothing out here of any real interest or purpose – no shops, no houses, just dust and grass.

This was the fact that bothered Leighton the most.

If there had been some nearby houses or an old ranch perhaps, he would have felt better. That would have meant that kid he had seen could perhaps have been running towards home – perhaps late for supper. Or if there had been a couple of residential homes nearby, it would have seemed possible that they were playing some game with friends. But there were no homes, no farms, not even a single building in sight.

It didn't seem right.

He reluctantly climbed back into the car. Annie glanced up from the pages.

'What's going on?' she asked.

'Nothing, kiddo,' Leighton smiled. 'We are just heading home.'

'Before the fire reaches us?' she asked with a smile that suggested she was teasing him.

'Exactly,' Leighton said with an approving nod of his head.

14

The valley through which Tina was walking was a long dusty channel lined with neat rows of gnarled trees. This dip in the landscape extended for a couple of miles in every direction, like a shallow canyon. Although it was only September, the strange trees reminded Tina of the fake black ones people would often put in their yards at Halloween. Their colourless branches seemed to twist and intertwine as if frustrated by the lack of moisture. She knew that she didn't want to be out here among the trees when it got dark because Tina suspected that in darkness the branches would look very much like scrawny clawed hands reaching out of the ground in search of children. But Tina didn't need to worry about that; she had no intention of remaining out in the open, she just had to keep moving and somehow she would find shelter.

At that point in her long day, Tina had been walking through the hot landscape for almost two hours, she felt hungry and thirsty, but she had no other option than to keep going. Her mind had slipped into some primitive self-preservation mode, in which she thought only in narrow little areas. She did not allow herself to think about her mom or home because she knew it would only end with her sobbing on the ground. Neither did she allow herself to think about her dad. The last time she had seen him was two years earlier, when he had left in a cab for the airport. In the intervening years her memory of him had grown hazy, like the pictures on food wrappers left out in the sun too long.

She did, however, allow herself to think about school. That was safe because it was normal but didn't have the deep emotional pain that thinking about her home had. Therefore, as she stepped between the rows of gnarled trees, Tina pictured each person in her class; what they looked like, how they spoke and what they usually brought in their lunch box. She didn't like sitting with Sam Tuchi because he always had salami in his lunch and Tina didn't like the smell, but she loved sitting with Hannah Turner because her grandpa made her lunch. He always gave her way too much and she would share her peanut butter cups with anyone nearby. Tina liked Hannah's hair too – it was long and usually pleated in a braid that sat over her shoulder like a sleeping pet snake. Sometimes, Tina wished that she could have long hair like Hannah. But she knew that since her dad left them to go to Alaska, her mom had to do everything in the morning – getting showered, fixing breakfast and hurrying them both out into the car. That meant she would never have time to sit and twist Tina's hair into braids. She had tried doing it herself, but her fingers were just too small to grip the separate strands of hair.

Tina's meandering thoughts allowed her to traverse miles without being overly aware of it. They also kept her mind off her dry mouth and throbbing feet. But at least the temperature had gradually begun to ease. Above her head the Californian sky was starting to fade to orange. Soon the sun would be going down. This detail may have caused another child, like Suzy, to panic but Tina had already anticipated this and built it into her simple plan.

She figured if she could just find somewhere to hide for the night and rest, she could probably wait till morning and then go looking for help. Part of her didn't want to think about being out here in the darkness all alone because that would be scary. But she knew that being alone in the darkness was still safer than being with the stranger. Plus, she just needed to get through the night. If she fell asleep, the time would pass by without her even noticing. Then maybe – when the sun came back up – Tina could climb to the highest place she could find to get a view of any nearby homes or shops. By that time, the stranger would probably have given up looking for her. At least that's what she told herself.

Tina was, however, only seven years old and couldn't yet understand that she was being pursued by somebody who was entirely consumed by twisted desires – somebody who would never give up.

15

ngela knew it was probably futile but she couldn't stop herself from searching. The sick feeling in her stomach, which bordered on full helpless panic, would not subside. The most precious part of her life was missing, and yet she felt as if she was expected to sit at home and do nothing. Every part of her maternal instinct strained against this unnatural response. The ridiculously young-looking police officers who had stopped by three hours earlier had told Angela that she had to remain home just in case Tina returned, or if the police needed to contact her with any news.

When she looked horrified at the thought of simply waiting, the taller of the two officers tried to reassure Angela by stating that a dozen or so children were reported missing to Oceanside P.D. by panicking parents every week and almost all of them would turn up within twenty-four to forty-eight hours. However, he had then asked for a recent photograph of Tina and stated calmly that they would circulate a description of her to all units in the city. He added that there were over two hundred officers, so with that many eyes on the lookout, Tina would be found.

The words of the police officer were not sufficient to soothe Angela's increasing sense of panic and frustration. She had spent an agonising hour sitting on her small front porch, watching the world grow dark whilst her daughter remained missing.

Thankfully, Jackie Bucowiz had recognised the desperation in Angela's eyes, and kindly agreed to wait on her porch in place of her. This gesture meant Angela was free to climb into her battered old station wagon and drive slowly along the stretch of road on either side of her home. She had rolled both windows down and was crawling along the roadside calling her daughter's name.

Angela Blanchette's throat burned and her voice cracked from a combination of fatigue and fear as she threw her daughter's name into the night. The urge to cry was strong, but she fought it. To slump would be easy, but it wouldn't bring Tina home. So, Angela held her growing fear and guilt and pain to one side whilst she directed all of her energy into finding her lost baby.

The car rolled slowly forward in the failing light and Angela kept on calling.

At one point she realised that if Tina, hurt somewhere, heard her mother's voice and called back, the groaning engine would drown out her small response. This was why she decided to stop the car and clamber frantically out of the driver's seat. Stepping onto the warm road in her bare feet gave Angela a much-needed sense of stability. Gulping in the night air, she held on to the hood of the car and called once more.

'Tina, it's mom!' she yelled. 'Can you hear me, baby?'

When no response came, Angela walked weak-legged to the edge of the road and stared into the colourless abyss of the countryside. She called her daughter's name again. From somewhere in the gloom there was a small scuttling sound as a lizard scuttled through the bone-dry debris. Angela felt a momentary flicker of hope, but this was soon followed by plummeting despair as she realised the noise had come from smaller creatures than her child. She took a deep breath and stepped into the wilderness – moving like someone under a spell. Perhaps, she thought, if she just went a little deeper then she would have a greater chance of finding her daughter.

Angela had always possessed a good imagination – even as a child – but now it was a curse filling her mind with vivid images of her child caught in a million different horrors. She had to fight the compulsion to roar into the dark night in despair. Her body trembled with a flood of unexpended adrenalin.

It was a warm evening, but the sun was sinking and Tina was only wearing her shorts and T-shirt. Her mother knew that she had never been a kid who tolerated cold very well. Even as a baby, she would never settle whilst the air con was running, and now she was out there in the dark. Although there remained a much more frightening possibility, Angela Blanchette refused to let her mind go there. Without any real cognitive processing, she had simply committed to believe that her daughter was alive, because the alternative was too absolute a horror to contemplate. Even the momentary consideration of such a thing would rob her of everything. Instead, Angela forced herself back from the hood of the car. Then continued calling her daughter's name like a siren in the fading light.

16

Leighton and Annie were snuggled together on the couch with a soft blanket over their knees, watching cartoons on TV. Annie was already wearing her favourite yellow *Dora the Explorer* pyjamas, but had skilfully managed to delay bedtime by requesting to watch five more minutes of cartoons. But as he felt his daughter's head lean increasingly on his shoulder, Leighton knew she was ready for bed. He had let her have this treat as he knew that later in the week her grandparents would arrive to take her to stay over with them for a few days. It was a gesture which they made every couple of months, mainly it was to spend some time with Annie, but it was partly to give Leighton a little break. He both welcomed and hated it.

Whilst the characters on the TV enjoyed a celebratory feast of pastrami and ice-cream triple decker sandwiches, Leighton carefully picked up the remote and turned down the volume. Annie only stirred slightly, so he sat up and tucked the blanket beneath her legs wrapping her up. When she was awake and wrapped like this, they would both refer to her as a 'blanket burrito'. It was something he had done since she was a baby. Back then, wrapping his tiny daughter up had been a simpler process. It also helped her to sleep better knowing she was securely held.

Leighton eased himself away from his daughter and quietly stood up. Looking down at her curled blissfully on the sofa, he felt like leaving her there to sleep, but knew that might result in her waking up later confused and scared. Instead he padded through to her bedroom and switched on the moon-shaped nightlight. As he gazed around the walls, plastered with posters of unicorns and hand drawn castles, Leighton smiled. He wished he could let her live in a world of castles and fairy tales, rather than growing up to face a complex and often cruel world. He often felt that was what he actually wanted for himself.

He rolled back the *Peter Pan* cover on Annie's bed, then walked softly back to where she lay. As he scooped up his daughter in his arms, Leighton smiled after she groaned out a little sigh before instantly falling straight back into a heavy sleep.

He lay her down, kissed her forehead.

'Goodnight, princess.'

Stepping quietly away from Annie's bedroom door, Leighton faced another night on his own. He walked back to the sofa, picked up the remote and switched off the TV. He then padded into the kitchen, opened the refrigerator, pulled out some items and began to methodically make the following day's packed lunch for Annie.

Once all items were secured in his daughter's strawberry-shaped lunch box, Leighton placed it in the refrigerator and took out a bottle of beer. After carrying it through to his own bedroom, he switched on the small bedside light on his nightstand. Leighton sat the beer next to his radio. Sitting on the bed, he switched on the radio and felt his muscles soften as the simple sound of Delta blues filled the room. The music reminded him of his father. As a younger man that had been enough to put Leighton off listening to such crackling old tunes, but now as he approached his fortieth birthday, he was beginning to grow more like his father in more ways than one.

After taking a shower Leighton dressed in crisp white boxer shorts and returned to his room. He then twisted the cap of his beer, took a sip and then lay back on the bed. Closing his eyes he let the sound of the music wash over him, and – for a little while – life was good.

17

A t the same time as her mother was calling into the indifferent darkness, Tina had made a discovery. The sinking sun had only just slipped behind the fading violet horizon, as the exhausted girl reached an area where the ground beneath her feet began to slope downwards. This incline made moving through the darkening landscape easier. Tina held on to brittle branches for support as she made her slow descent. Her tired muscles had little left to give, and so simply allowed the girl to stumble down the slope, kicking up small puffs of dust with her feet. Halfway down, she lost one of her shoes entirely, but she was too exhausted to retrieve it. Instead, she shambled endlessly down the hill until she found herself standing on more level ground in a small valley flanked on three sides by tree covered hills.

It was here in the shadow of this valley that Tina found herself facing a cluster of old farm buildings. The angular structures were old and wooden, odd curls of defiant paint on the otherwise colourless planks suggested the place had once been painted yellow, but decades of exposure to the elements had bleached them. A dusty track, which may have once served as a road, led out of the cluster of buildings and stretched off into the flat darkness beyond.

When she first glimpsed the area, Tina had initially believed that the place might be occupied and perhaps some friendly old lady would take her inside, and then call Tina's mother on the telephone to come and collect her. But upon closer inspection, Tina realised that the place seemed dark and lifeless. Yet, the sour sweet tang of citrus fruit hung in the air like the ghost of some far away summer. The smell reminded Tina of a car air freshener her mom had once got when she got new tyres fitted on her car. It had been in the shape of a small tree but instead of being green it was orange. Tina had really liked the scent at first, but eventually it started to make her feel sick – especially on longer car journeys, like when they went to visit her Aunt Susan over in Barstow.

Although she didn't know it, Tina had stumbled into a disused orange processing plant, which had been abandoned since the year of her birth. The Pembleton Farm Fruit Company had offered up eight years of sweet liquid before finally closing down when two seasons of canker killed off almost all the trees. The three buildings had once served as an office, a washroom and a wooden pump house.

Despite her fear of the silent old buildings, Tina edged towards them in the gloom. In her mind she recalled the story of *Goldilocks and the Three Bears* and hoped that she might find some safety within the dried-up walls. Perhaps there might even be a telephone. She knew her home number – mom had taught her it the previous summer – and could easily dial 911 to ask for help. But as she stepped ever closer to the looming buildings it became clear to Tina that they were little more than dried-up shapes, like an old packing crate she had once found washed up on Buccaneer Beach. The memory of that day, when she and her mom had splashed in the foamy waves and made squishy footprints in the damp sand, caused an emotional pain in Tina that threatened to overwhelm her. But, much like her faraway mother, she knew she could not – *must not* – let that happen. She pushed the memory aside and focused on the possibility that the stranger was still out there following her.

Tina felt a new sense of a more immediate fear start to form deep within her stomach. She didn't want to approach the cluster of buildings with all those empty black windows from which anything, or anyone, might be looking. To the left there was a flat roofed office building, bleached by countless summers. In the middle was what appeared to be a roofless toilet block, and to the right was a larger barn-like structure. All of them looked to Tina like something she'd seen in an episode of *Scooby-Doo*. Yet despite her fear, she knew that she needed to rest. Her feet were blistered and stinging at the heel where the back of her small shoes were cutting into the skin, but even still she was hesitant. Then she saw something in the fading light that made her rush over to the office. A few feet along from the door, protruding from the wall was a brass faucet. There was a grubby plastic tub on the dusty ground beneath it. Tina had half expected the rough-edged container to be brimming with water, but as she peered into it she discovered that the tub was empty except for a couple of old beer bottles and a dead bug. Turning her attention to the faucet, Tina licked her lips. It had been five hours since she had last had a drink. In the intervening hours she had crossed eleven miles on foot beneath a scorching sun. Gripping the faucet, Tina tried twisting it. The faucet was stiff and the effort hurt her small hands, but desperation kept her going and the faucet began to turn. There was a gurgle, as if some underground troll was chuckling at Tina's hopeless situation, then a sudden splash of water came out in a belching splatter. It was not the steady stream of water she would have seen at home; instead this was an irregular flow, sloshing into the plastic tub. Tina cupped her hand into the flowing water and scooped some to her dry lips. It tasted warm, but clean. Within seconds she had put her mouth to the faucet and gulped down mouthfuls. When she was done drinking, Tina decided that she definitely should bring some water with her. She reached into the plastic tub and fished out one of the old bottles and a discarded lid. Having poured out its contents, she filled the bottle then twisted the faucet shut again. Finally, caked in dust and bottle in hand like a small town drunk, Tina Blanchette decided that she desperately needed to find a place to rest for the night. First of all she decided to try the building marked 'office'.

Pushing the door open, Tina got a real fright as some small hidden creature scampered away from her and deeper into the dark labyrinth. Suppressing a scream, Tina stepped instinctively back from the rectangle of darkness, and then peered into the void. She waited, frozen, listening to the sound of her own heartbeat. Tilting her head to one side, the small girl suddenly heard the dry rustling noise of something scuttling through the darkness. As she thought of the possible explanations for such a sound – lizards, snakes or perhaps large spiders – Tina realised that no matter how afraid she was of the stranger, it would be impossible for her to enter into that place. Instead, she hurried over to the bulky silhouette of the barn structure. It was long, but even in the low light, Tina could see that it had a large square opening at both ends. That was good. It meant she could escape if she needed to. And so she stepped into the building, but rather than feeling afraid of the shadows, she felt some comfort in them. At least her choice meant she was in some sort of physical place. If her mom had told the police to look for her, they would probably look in places like this, rather than in endless fields and hills.

Gazing around the barn in the gloom, Tina thought about simply finding a corner to lie down in and wait for morning. But she imagined that the dusty corners might attract the very creatures she was afraid of, and so she made a brave decision. Tina decided to get as high up off the ground as she could. There was some form of u-shaped ledge running around the inner walls of the building about twelve or so feet off the ground. Tina knew the approximate height because it looked a little higher than her own roof at home. Her mom had told her that was eleven feet high.

Something resembling a huge ribbon of dark fabric extended from the ceiling to the floor, brushing past the narrow upper floor. The material- which was at least as wide as a person- reminded Tina of the moving belt that her mom placed the groceries on in the supermarket. For a moment, Tina felt so exhausted that she considered curling up behind this large strip of material. But she knew that she wouldn't be safe there if the stranger came looking for her. Instead, she moved toward it and touched the fabric. It felt rough like an old tent that her class had once used during a school project on famous explorers. They had set it up at the back of the classroom, and adorned it with pictures of creatures found in the Amazon Jungle. Tina liked the tent, but had been surprised by how scratchy the material felt whenever she touched it.

She glanced upwards at the ledge, then all around the vast space. Even in the colourless gloom, Tina could see there were no stairs leading up to relative safety. But the increasing darkness motivated her to find a solution.

Tina then pushed her water bottle into the waistband of her shorts, gripped the rough material and began to climb upwards. Her feet burned as she pressed them flat against the fabric and scrambled frantically towards the upper level. She almost slipped a couple of times, but her survival instinct was strong. Despite the exhaustion and her burning muscles, the small girl continued her ascent.

Eventually, Tina reached the upper level and grazed her knees clambering on to the flat surface. Having reached the top, she knelt on the wood, pulled the bottle from her shorts and took a sip. She peered around and realised then that it was simply a balcony which ran all the way around the building. In one corner of it a wide ribbon of the same coarse material she had climbed up was coiled like a giant snake skin. Tina walked unsteadily towards it. Then in a daze of physical and emotional exhaustion, she placed her bottle upon the dusty wooden floor and sat down. She pulled at the material until it covered her legs, then placed her head on her hands.

It was there in the dark folds of the old conveyor belt that Tina Blanchette curled like a small mammal and silently the cried herself to sleep.

18

The stranger pulled up outside his home on the outer rim of the trailer park and climbed out of his vehicle. It had taken him almost an hour and a half to find his way back to his parked car, then an additional half hour to drive home. He was exhausted and had not eaten in hours. Throughout the journey he had been overcome by emotions and had slipped in and out of the present time, sometimes thinking that he still had the girl in trunk of his car and he was driving her to his home. This was hardly surprising – he had been rehearsing this event in his mind for days.

At one point, just outside the city limits, he pulled off the freeway and on to a lonely side road. After driving along the track for half a mile, he found a place to stop. With the lights switched off, nobody else would see his car out here. He got out of the car then stumbled through the dust to the rear of it. Lifting open the trunk, he closed his eyes and made a desperate wish that she would still be in there, curled like a frightened kitten in the dark.

The loss he felt by staring into the empty trunk was almost unbearable for him. After glancing around to ensure that he would not be seen by passing cars, the stranger climbed inside the trunk and lay curled in the space the girl had earlier occupied. He started off by sobbing quietly, but within moments he began to roll from side to side moaning and then increasing the movement until he was thrashing around. His balled fists punched the inside of the cavity in a relentless frenzy. The crazed motion was enough to cause the car to rock from side to side. He only stopped when a passing car slowed down. The stranger lay in the dark, breathing heavily, listening to the approaching vehicle. If the car stopped and the driver came over to discover him lying, raging in the trunk, it would be necessary to take some action. As he waited, the stranger's bleeding fist moved instinctively to the hunting knife kept on his belt. Thankfully, the driver of the approaching car changed his mind, and sped up. The stranger sighed as the sound of the vehicle faded into the night.

***

After climbing up the five steps, the stranger pushed his key in the door lock. His was a 1985 wide trailer. He had paid extra for it, not for the additional width but for the fact that the internal floor level was four feet higher than the ground. This meant that the substantial crawl space beneath the structure was enclosed on all sides by a cinder block wall.

Having turned the lock, the stranger entered the trailer, and felt a tide of rage wash over him. This should have been his moment of bliss, he should have been returning home with a secret treat in the trunk of his car. He had planned to arrive home, have a drink to celebrate and then, once the other trailers fell silent for the night, he would transfer the kid. Now his plans were ruined.

Closing the door of his trailer, he turned and looked at the living area. Two mismatched sofas formed an L-shape around a small coffee table. The table was square and sat on top of a zebra-print rug. A couple of car magazines were randomly spread on top of the table. There was also a copper ashtray, a half empty bag of potato chips and an empty beer bottle. The scene looked fairly low-key and natural, but that was the whole point of the display. The stranger walked across the room to the table and lifted it up. None of the items on top of it moved. They were all attached to the surface with superglue – even the magazines. This would allow him to quickly replace the table if anyone ever came to his door.

Once he had placed the table to one side, he turned his attention to the woollen rug. Kneeling down on the wood-effect flooring, he slowly peeled the rug off the floor. The Velcro tape which held the rug securely in place tore apart from itself to reveal a neatly marked square in the centre of the floor. Inside the outline of Velcro was a square wooden hatch. The edges of this square were raw and splintered where the circular saw had ripped through the flooring, when the stranger had created it.

Once he had discarded the rug, the stranger then knelt down in front of the hatch and reached under his T-shirt. He pulled out the sheath knife that had been jammed into his waist band. Gripping the leather sheath in his left hand, the stranger slid the blade out and inserted it into the edge of the hatch. Bearing down on the knife, he levered the hatch open an inch, then pushed his fingers into the gap he had created. He grunted as he lifted the hatch fully open. Shuffling around and mumbling to himself, the stranger manoeuvred himself so that his legs were dangling over the edge of the dark square space. He placed his hands, palm-down on either side of the opening then, like someone sinking into a hole cut on a frozen lake, lowered himself down into the darkness.

For a moment he clattered around in the shadows until a flare from his zippo lighter ignited a flame which was passed between a couple of wax candles which were stuck in the earth floor. The sickly flickering light illuminated an underground chamber which was almost half the size of the trailer above. It was large enough for the stranger to move around in on all fours. The side walls of the crawl space had originally been formed by the cinder blocks of the supports for the structure above, but the stranger had modified them. Over a period of three weeks he had carefully lined each of the four outer walls with insulated tiles. The first ones he had picked up from Home Depot had been too large to fit through the hatch, so he had returned them and replaced them with smaller ones that were rectangular and just slim enough to fit through the square hole in the trailer floor. These tiles had been stuck to the original blocks, creating a second inner wall. The main benefit of this part of the project had been to soundproof the place, but the addition of the foil backed tiles also meant that the temperature down here remained fairly constant. He figured that might have been useful if he kept somebody in here during the winter months. In a few places the stranger had stuck pictures from kids' comics on to the walls. He didn't have masking tape so he had attached the pictures of cartoon bears and unicorns with three inch masonry nails. The stranger crawled across the subterranean chamber to the corner furthest away from the hatch. This was his favourite part of his underground bunker; a small steel cage waiting to be filled. It had originally been designed for use with a dog, but like the outside walls, the stranger had modified it. He used an angle grinder to cut it into sections that would allow them to fit through the hatch. He then rebuilt in the glaring light of an arc welder. The final addition was a thick padlock.

As he reached the square structure, the stranger felt himself fizz with excitement. The following day, if he did things properly, he could recapture the girl and bring her here – to her new home.

19

ngela was lost in the warm dark waters of sleep. Her eyelids twitched as she dreamt of her child. In the fantasy, she and Tina had been holding each other's hands as they wandered through some ethereal city. The ornate buildings forming a labyrinth around them were tall and vague, fading into the heavens. They also curved upwards at angles which were only possible in the formless geometry of dreams. One of Tina's small hands held on to her mother like a small clamp; the other held a pink cloud of cotton candy wrapped around a thin wooden stick. The situation felt happy to Angela, but some dark menace was already starting to form at the fringes of her consciousness. She sensed that this comforting vision was not, in fact, reality. Yet she still held on to her daughter's small, warm hand – absorbing the sense of connection no matter how illusionary it might be.

But at some point in the dream, things began to change. A sudden gust of wind whipped the cotton candy up into the air and sent it whirling away like a small pink tornado into the darkening sky. Even in the vagueness of the dream, Angela felt a shudder of panic as her daughter quickly slipped her fingers free from her mother's grasp and ran off in pursuit of the treat. Angela called after the child and tried to move after her, but her legs refused to respond. She looked down to see that her bare feet had been fastened to the sidewalk by large twisted nails.

Angela gasped in the darkness and her eyes sprang open. She was still dressed in her faded jeans and T-shirt. The latter was soaked with sweat and clung to her back like a second skin. Her instinct was to clamber out of bed and run to her daughter's dark bedroom, but the realization that this would be pointless hit her like a physical blow. Her daughter was not in her room, or anywhere else in the house. She wasn't anywhere that Angela could reach her.

Rolling off the cheap mattress, Angela was running on autopilot as her hand fluttered beneath her bed, grasping for her sneakers. Having located them, she slipped them on to her feet.

Then, for a moment, Angela sat on the edge of her bed, holding her hot face in her hands, trying simply to breathe. But in that instant, panic flooded her system, and she could feel the adrenalin compelling her muscles to action. Despite the infuriating advice telling her to do nothing other than wait, Angela knew as a mother she had to do something to help her baby.

After hurrying downstairs, Angela left the door unlocked as it clattered shut behind her. Fumbling with the keys, she unlocked her grey Toyota and climbed inside. It was then, sitting in the darkness of her driveway, that great heaving sobs overwhelmed Angela Blanchette like a dark wave. She gripped the steering wheel with both hands and wept relentlessly. Eventually, when the tears started to subside, she felt a wave of nausea flood her. Her hand flapped around seeking the handle of the door. When she found it, Angela flung the door open and leaned out. The vomit rose in her and fell upon the ground in wet splatter. She stayed in that position, holding the door for support, until the nausea finally subsided.

Angela sat back in the car, and used the back of her hand to wipe the acidic liquid from her face. Her throat burned, and she was barely aware of the hot tears flooding her cheeks. As the sobbing took over, her entire body shook with the force of the sense of loss. At one point, her crying was so strong that it made breathing difficult. Her breath came only in desperate gasps, which were punctuated by an agonising mantra of her daughter's name.

20

At roughly the same time as her mother was retching out of the driver side of the old Buick, Tina Blanchette awoke in the claustrophobic darkness of her own strange new home. At first, in the confusion of sleep, she initially thought she had fallen asleep in her garden, like the time the previous summer when she and her mother had lain on a makeshift bed in their garden to watch a meteor shower. They had placed an old inflatable mattress on the ground and covered it with blankets and quilts. Lying beneath the stars was both adventurous and magical. However, a late supper of grilled cheese and hot chocolate meant that, despite her desire to see the stars, Tina had fallen asleep and awoken beneath the sparkling stars to find her mother curled around her like a contented cat. Instead of waking her mom, Tina had pulled the quilt and blankets over them both and cuddled in.

But this felt different from the garden, and even as the last tendrils of sleep faded away, she knew something was not right. The air was too cool and the sounds of the insects too loud to be the garden of her small neat home.

Tina rubbed her eyes and then pulled her knees up to her chin. It took her a moment to remember where she was. Perhaps this was because she ultimately didn't want to accept the horror of her situation, or perhaps the situation was simply too strange to accept. It took a while for Tina's eyes to adjust. The vault of the attic was long and dark. The area at the far end formed a triangle of darkness in which all sorts of horrors might be hiding. Sitting fully upright, she peered into the blackness, and blinked her eyes to try to make it more distinct. It didn't work. The darkness was so complete that it appeared almost solid. Yet it seemed to be spreading, seeping towards her like oil in water. It was as if she was sitting before a black hole as it spread outwards, threatening to engulf everything in its path. Unable to take her eyes away, she watched in fascinated horror as the darkness expanded, unfolding like some huge black flower.

Annie felt that if she looked away this expanding void would reach her and consume her. At that point, frozen with fear she wished that she had remained outside – whatever the risks – amongst the clambering arms of the black trees. But wishing was futile. Her reality was absolute and immovable. All the wishing in the world wouldn't get her out of this pulsing world of spreading shadows.

Tina leaned her head against the wooden slats of the wall behind her, but kept her eyes fixed on the tumbling darkness. It was an almost defensive action – as if by actively observing she would somehow hold the restless darkness at bay. Eventually, inevitably exhaustion and emotional trauma overcame her and Tina Blanchette curled into the dark corner of the roof space and wept, face pressed against the arid beams, until she finally fell into a deep and troubled sleep.

21

It was a bright morning in Oceanside and the air coming in from the ocean smelled clean and fresh. But even in the crystal clarity of the coastal air, there was a hint of wood smoke drifting down like a ghost from the occasional wildfires on the distant hills. At 8am it was still early enough in the morning that the sound of traffic on the highway was not yet sufficiently loud to mask the distant sound of waves crashing into themselves.

Leighton got out of his car in the staff parking area at the rear of the station. This was a small parking lot where some older vehicles were sprinkled amongst work cruisers. Behind a single chain-link fence were a number of impounded cars – old and new – all of which were in better condition than Leighton's battered old jalopy. He mostly parked next to them. Some of the other traffic officers joked that Leighton chose this spot because he hoped that one day his car would be mistaken for an unclaimed impounded one and be towed away to the junkyard. They could not have been more wrong.

As it was, he felt too affectionate towards the old car to ever get rid of it. It had been the only car Annie had ever known – the one that carried her from the hospital to her home. It had been the one all three of them had shared when they had briefly been an okay family. The back seat still featured the sunken lines where Annie's infant seat had been positioned for three years, the trunk contained the sandy crumbs from a thousand days at the beach, and the glove box – like some sunken treasure chest – still faithfully held a selection of Heather's favourite CDs.

All of this made the car more of a memory box than a vehicle. Therefore, the real reason he parked at the rear of the station next to the bangers rather than out front, was that he knew that – like him – it looked a mess but was good on the inside. He just didn't want to have to explain that to anybody else. Here amongst the junk, there was less chance of that.

As Leighton made his way into the building, he passed by the locker area, where Officer Danny Clarke was sitting down on a varnished wooden bench and polishing one of his black shoes. He was wearing it on his hand like a strange glove as he rubbed at some persistent stain with a bright orange rag.

'Hey, Danny,' Leighton said with a smile, 'you getting yourself all fresh for the beautiful day ahead?'

The other officer glanced up and nodded sagely.

'Sure am, Jonesy. Can't patrol the highways without some gleaming footwear, can I?'

'No, not according to the last uniform directive I read,' Leighton said and pointed to a notice on a cork pin board on a corner wall. It had been issued the previous month and instructed all officers on expected standards of uniform whilst on duty.

Danny chuckled and slipped on his shoe and began tying his laces.

'Well I guess I'm just about ready to face the public. Hey, I meant to ask how things were working out with your rookie.'

'You've heard, I take it?' Leighton asked with a crooked smile.

'Nothing official.' Danny shrugged. 'But you know what this place is like – everyone says he's up to the same old snitching game with you too. Sounds like Teddy doesn't take well to experienced officers, huh?'

'No, he does not. I think he's made six complaints about me – that's just the ones I know about. Can you believe that?'

'Six is nothing, Jonesy – I had chalked up eleven by the time I was finally relieved of that particular babysitting duty.'

'Did you request the move?' Leighton asked, suddenly interested in the possibility of liberating himself.

'Actually, I did – on three separate occasions, but that isn't what got the rookie off my back.'

'What did then?'

'I guess the captain finally got pissed off having to wipe Teddy's ass at the end of every watch. But I don't care – it all worked out in the end. He's with a more experienced officer than me.' Danny winked.

'Yeah, well I guess your gain is my loss,' Leighton said with a gracious nod as he moved towards the hallway leading to the administration area.

'Hey, sorry about that,' Danny called after him. He sounded genuinely repentant, 'I didn't get any say in who he got placed with.'

'Don't worry about it, Danny,' Leighton shrugged, 'Teddy is the least of my troubles.'

***

As he entered the bustling office area, Leighton made his way to a small cluttered booth located at the rear of the room. Even though it was only eight-nineteen in the morning, there were already several officers answering calls or faceting information into bulky ivory collared typewriters.

Leighton eased himself into his temperamental office chair, opened a deep drawer and removed a white incident form. After placing the paper flat on the desk, he rummaged around for a reliable pen. Whilst Leighton did this, his eyes slid over the various photos pinned around his booth – Annie as a baby, wrapped in blanket, Annie on the first day of school, and his favourite, Annie peering into a rock pool over at the Strand Beach.

He tried to avoid looking at the images too intently. If he did, Leighton could easily be overcome by a sudden rising panic that his daughter was someplace else – somewhere he couldn't protect her. At such times, his body was flooded with adrenalin, and he would rush out to the parking lot where he would pace forwards and backwards until the feeling abated. One afternoon ten weeks earlier, when had been due to take a 'Driver Awareness' class for six DUI felons, he had been unable to walk the rising panic away and he actually left the station, climbed in his car and drove to Annie's school.

When he pulled up in his car on the opposite side of the street, Leighton found that his arrival at the school coincided with recess and Annie was happily running around the playground with her friends. Luckily, she never saw him, otherwise Leighton wouldn't have known what to tell her.

As he drove back to the station that morning, he resolved to keep his anxieties away from his daughter. Regardless how uncomfortable his own feelings got, he would just have to endure them. But his absence from work that morning had not gone unnoticed. When he returned to work, he was taken into a side room and given a written reprimand from Captain Pierce. Slightly worse was the fact that following the incident some of the other officers would silently stare at him as he passed by in the locker room, as if at any moment he might run off to save his daughter from imaginary threats. It didn't bother Leighton too much; he figured they were probably right.

***

Leighton took his notepad from his chest pocket and flipped the cover open to reveal his account of the previous afternoon. He had intended to submit his paper report before clocking off the watch the previous evening, but he had been in a hurry to collect Annie, so he had simply grabbed a form from the numerous shelves in the office and slipped it into his drawer. Three months earlier the district had rolled out a proactive approach called 'Policing for Prevention'. This included a number of community activities and an increase in beat cops in certain neighbourhoods, but it also required that all police incident reports were submitted within twenty-four hours of the incident occurring. Leighton could see the sense in it but that didn't stop it being a pain in the ass when trying to reach his child-minder before nightfall.

Not being particularly adept at using a computer or at filling in forms, Leighton looked at the future of policing as looking increasingly administrative, and that was a frightening prospect.

***

Leighton had only just completed filling in the form when he became aware of somebody behind him. He turned to see Teddy standing with his arms folded.

'I've been waiting out in the cruiser since quarter past,' he said.

'Yeah?' Leighton grabbed his paper work and stood up. 'Well I guess you must be pretty keen to get started today.'

'Our watch starts at eight thirty. We should be on the road by now.'

'I get that, Teddy,' Leighton said, calmly, 'I just needed to fill in a report on that RTA from yesterday.'

'That report should've been submitted last night.'

'Yeah? Well it's done now.' Leighton stood up. 'I guess it's just a little late.' Leighton said with a shrug. He then sauntered slowly across the room to where the wire baskets for various reports were lined up on a long metal desk. In a move that was intentionally designed to irritate Teddy further, Leighton deliberately placed his paperwork into the wrong basket. 'Okay, that's the fun stuff over,' he said with a smile, 'let's go to work, partner.' Teddy said nothing but turned and walked out of the room.

As Leighton crossed the parking lot, walking slightly behind Teddy who was striding purposefully to their designated cruiser, he caught the eye of Danny Clarke loading stacks of orange road cones into the open trunk of his own vehicle.

He grinned and offered a thumbs up to Leighton who responded by silently mouthing 'thanks' and flicking a middle finger.

Danny laughed and busied himself with his work.

22

The stranger made his way stealthily through the wide field of dry grass on the northern side of Old Mill Way. Drifting slowly in his colourless clothes among the lingering wisps of mist, he looked like a scarecrow that had somehow come to life and clambered down from his perch. It was still early in the morning, but he had awoken with a sense of urgency – partly as a result of the last time he had been forced to leave a kid – that he was compelled to seek out the girl. Even though the temperature was still relatively cool, the stranger was already soaked with sweat, and his damp hair hung across his eyes in greasy strands which he regularly had to brush aside.

Being out the wild like this was both problematic and beneficial for the stranger. It was difficult terrain to navigate; several months without rain had left the ground compacted and hard. In addition to that, when he finally found the girl he would have to leave her body behind rather than risk carrying it all the way back to civilisation. On the plus side, the pursuit was not impossible, he knew that the girl couldn't have gone far, particularly on such uneven ground. But there were places to hide out here, especially for kids. That meant that he would have to think from her point of view – see the place through her eyes if he was to locate her before anybody else did. It would be a fun game. In any case, there was nowhere to get food or water out here, so even if he couldn't find the girl all he needed to do was keep her from getting back to civilisation and she would shrivel away to nothing like a raisin under the hot sun.

Stepping through the arid ground, he occasionally stopped and remained utterly still. At such times he slowed his breathing and closed his eyes. He would listen as all of the sounds around him – the chirp and creak of insects, the song of lonely birds in the nearby trees – began to fade into nothingness. Then he would feel himself no longer as a man, but as something more – or less. He became everything and nothing. This moment of meditation gave him the clarity he needed to consider his next move, without his thoughts being clouded by emotions. Whenever he came back to reality, he felt refreshed and carried on his grim journey with a renewed sense of purpose.

He had started his journey by entering the countryside at the place where he knew the girl had escaped. However, given the earlier presence of the cop, he didn't want to leave his car parked at the edge of the road in case it drew any unwanted attention, so he had left it back at the trailer and took a cab ride instead.

Once he was away from the road, he started walking in a very deliberate direction. He followed the easiest path, knowing that a desperate person running from a threat would most likely opt for the easiest path to safety – at least that's what he would do. He doubted that a seven-year-old kid would be any different, but it was possible. The landscape did little to support the stranger in his quest. The ground was too baked to absorb any footprints and the entire area was dotted with trees and long grass. There was no sign of a specific path. And yet he continued undeterred. The prize was too great to give up.

The low flatland eventually began to sweep up on to a gentle slope that was studded with more trees and cacti. The stranger figured that this hillside must have had more water in it than the surrounding area to support the increased amount of growth here. This incline became gradually steeper, causing him to slow his pace.

Eventually, after walking for a little over three hours, he found what he had been looking for. He had reached the top of the hill, and gazed down on a small valley. A wide grin spread across the stranger's face. He found himself looking at a small cluster of run-down buildings. They would provide the perfect place for a kid to take shelter for the night.

The stranger licked his lips and then began creeping quietly down the slope towards the structures.

23

The burning sensation in Tina's lower stomach had been steadily increasing since she had awoken in the cool light of dawn, cold and disoriented. She felt as if she didn't pee soon, she would have no choice. Her first instinct was simply to climb down from her perch and run off in any direction. But part of her – the part that she was trying to listen to – understood that the stranger might have spent the night nearby, and be sitting… waiting. Tina sighed, pulled the rough canvas tightly around her and sobbed quietly. Gradually, the pain in her bladder subsided enough that she could partly ignore it.

However, the sensation returned a couple of times. But when it came back for a third time it was at a level of intensity Tina could no longer ignore. She knew it would be impossible to wait until darkness to go pee. But the risk didn't seem too great.

All she needed to do was drop the large coils of the belt, descend it and then quickly scamper off into the long grass. If she could make the trip in the blackness of night out here, she could easily do it during daytime – maybe even running for part of the way. And yet despite the simplicity of her plan, Tina was not entirely certain that the stranger had gone. She kept a silent vigil, peeking through the gaps and knotholes in the corner. She moved her eyes from plank to plank, searching the golden landscape for any sign of threat.

Eventually, she realised that she was being dumb. The stranger was likely miles away. She concluded that the odds were in her favour.

She took one last glance through the gap in the wooden slats which served as a wall for the upper level of the structure. Seeing no sign of the stranger, Tina slid her empty beer bottle into her belt, then quickly pushed the old conveyor belt off the platform until it hung in the air like a hung snake skin. Tina leaned out from the platform and grabbed the material with both hands. Gripping tightly, she swung her body out to meet the belt. The move reminded Tina of something she did in her gym class. Moving silently, hand under hand, down to the ground, Tina made slow progress. She then carefully peeked out of the barn and, seeing no sign of life, ran into the long grass.

The relief Tina felt was unbelievable. Crouching in the long grass, her urine hissed on the parched mud and, by the time she was buttoning back up her shorts, had already been absorbed. Tina took a moment to survey her environment. Glancing around at the surrounding landscape, the area seemed flatter and wider than it had seemed the previous evening. Behind the building she had taken refuge in, Tina could see the large hill she had descended the previous evening. The ground in front of the buildings was covered in trees, and stretched off to meet the distant horizon. Tina narrowed her eyes and peered through the trunks, hoping to find some distant house or some indication of life, but she saw nothing but dry land.

In the process of moving she decided it would be a good idea to fill up her bottle with water before thinking about what to do next. However, as she turned back to face the buildings, she froze.

She was already half standing when she found herself looking directly at the stranger's back.

'Tina!' he bellowed toward the buildings. 'You in there, honey?'

He was standing a few feet outside of her temporary home, staring directly at it. Tina almost fainted at the sight of him, but somehow the horror seemed to keep her fully conscious out of fear. Instead of collapsing, she sank slowly back into the long grass, but never once moved her eyes off the stranger. He looked older than she initially had thought. But was still wearing the same grubby clothes, except he had added a baseball cap with some letter logo on it. In one hand he held some twisted piece of metal attached to a piece of rope that was coiled over his shoulder. The rope looked old and colourless, as if he had found it in one of the other buildings. Tina thought that he looked like he was going looking for the world's biggest fish.

She kept perfectly still, crouched in the dust and watched him as he moved around the outside of the building, peering up at it. The fact that he was no longer calling out to her suggested to Tina that he was confident that he had found her hiding place.

'Tina!' he called again. 'I just need to talk to you, about getting you back home.'

Tina's eyes remained fixed on him, but when the stranger stepped into the shadow of the building she pushed herself carefully on to her hands and knees. This position allowed her to watch in horror as the stranger stood inside the structure. After gazing around at the walls and roof he took a couple of steps over to the pit, and tilted his head downwards. Tina figured he must be checking to see if she had fallen down there. When he was done, the stranger turned his attention to the upper floor. He dropped the rope from his shoulder on to the ground. After crouching down beside it, he began to tie several knots along the length of the rope. Once he was done, the stranger stood up again. Gripping the metal hook in one hand, he began swinging the rope around like some sort of rodeo cowboy. After whirling it in the air for a moment, the stranger would regularly throw it up on to the platform above his head. At first Tina thought he was trying to use it as grapple like in the *Batman* movies that her next-door neighbour watched endlessly. But at the start, the stranger seemed to be making no attempt to climb anything. He just kept swinging it up on to the upper floor then he would pull on the rope again. Tina figured that the anchor must not have fastened to anything because it came clattering back down. The stranger cursed as he did this and had to jump out of the way a couple of times. On one occasion he stepped back and after standing on his tiptoes, he jumped up in the air as if trying to get a better view of what was up there. He then picked the hook up again and swung it up onto the first floor. This time when he pulled in the rope it didn't move. The stranger wiped his sweating forehead with the back of his hand, then wiped both hands on the legs of his jeans. He then reached up, gripped the rope with both hands and began to climb it.

Tina considered using that moment, whilst the stranger was on the upper platform, to stand up and run like a mouse when the cat is looking away. But then she remembered how easily she had been able to see through the gaps in the wooden slats. That meant if she stood up and moved anywhere, the stranger would be able to see her. Then he would surely jump off the platform and come after her.

So, she cowered in the dust and waited, hoping that she would not be visible from inside the structure.

After a long time, the stranger emerged from the barn. Tina thought he couldn't have been up on the platform all that time, so perhaps he had climbed down into the pit to see if she was hiding among the machinery. As he stepped into the sunlight, Tina could see that the stranger's face was shining with sweat and his T-shirt looked like it was sticking to him.

Tina held her breath, terrified that he would come looking for her in the grass, but thankfully he didn't. Instead he walked tentatively into the shadowy entrance of the office building.

Tina heard the sound of more clattering coming from inside that building. He was inside for a long time, and Tina began to worry that he was planning on staying there. However, after half an hour he emerged again from the dark doorway. His face and clothes were streaked with sweat and dust. He peered around the landscape for a few minutes then glanced at his watch. It was then that he walked around the side of the barn a couple of times and then finally began climbing back up the slope of the large hill.

Even though, at that point, the stranger had his back to her, Tina didn't dare move from her hiding place. She watched as the figure on the hillside grew smaller and smaller, as if he'd taken the shrinking potion from *Alice in Wonderland*. Even when he vanished over the distant edge of the crest of the hill, Tina remained in the same place.

Eventually, when she felt happy that the stranger was far enough away, Tina darted out of the grass and ran to the water faucet. After switching it on, she lapped at it like a dog, before filling up her glass bottle.

She then tucked the glass bottle into the waistband of her shorts, turned and ran as fast as she could away from the buildings and the looming hill behind her.

24

The stranger trudged sullenly back through the hot landscape in the vague direction of his car. Although he was empty-handed, his journey had not been entirely fruitless. He knew the kid had been there – the water in the basin beneath the faucet confirmed that she had been there at least once and he felt in his bones that she was still there too. The area of scrubland in front of the buildings stretched for miles north-west. It was flat unforgiving terrain, peppered with cacti, dried bushes and occasional trees. If the girl had headed off that way, she would most likely be dead already. The journey on foot would be difficult enough for an adult with supplies to make; it would be impossible for a kid.

The buildings had all been empty, but that didn't mean they hadn't offered shelter to the girl. He cursed himself for not being more patient. When he discovered the place he should have remained hidden and waited until dark. Then he could have come across her as she slept. But he had gone and drawn attention to himself, and hadn't found her.

If she was still in the area and was hiding, then that meant she had been smart enough to hide. That was a development that made his task trickier, but he enjoyed the challenge.

When he had been in the dusty old office, the stranger had found an old print on the wall that showed an older ranch with the same hill above it. Beneath it were the words *Pembleton Farm*. He made a note of it, knowing he could use this to find a map of the place – identify any potential hiding places. Then he would draw up a plan before returning to lure the girl out. He figured it shouldn't be too difficult. If she had been out there for a couple of days with nothing to eat or drink then food and maybe some soda might be enough to tempt her into the open.

He decided that he would go back the following morning, set a trap and catch her like a young rabbit in a snare.

25

After walking for more than two hours, wearing only one worn-out shoe, Tina Blanchette was really struggling to stay upright. Her journey away from the barn had taken her through the veil of trees and onto a flat and relatively featureless plane. Behind her, the hill and buildings had gradually shrunk as she pushed steadily forward. However, the area in front of her seemed to stretch into infinity. Limping onwards, Tina was near to collapsing from exhaustion. The impact on her body of the earlier day's journey was much greater than she thought. Her muscles ached from the miles she had covered, and the friction from the strap of her one remaining sandal had caused a painful blister to form on the back of her foot, but she was reluctant to give the shoe up because the ground was covered in so many sharp stones.

The scorching heat of the oppressive sun was so strong that it felt like a physical weight pressing down on her shoulders. Eventually, this painful burden slowed her lumbering pace to a stop.

She wiped the sticky sweat from her eyes, then lifted the old beer bottle to her cracked lips. As it tilted in the air, the brown glass bottle was flooded with light, and, for a moment, Tina looked like a tiny angel blowing on a celestial trumpet. But the final drops of water were warm and not sufficient to hydrate the girl's burning throat. She swallowed them but the sensation felt dry and painful.

Tina swayed to one side like a small drunk, then let the bottle slip from her sweaty grasp. Made brittle by the elements, it landed on a rock and detonated into glittering fragments of splintered glass.

Glancing down absently at the ragged remains of her bottle lying in the dusty ground, Tina wanted to cry, but had neither the energy nor the water for tears.

Instead, she drifted sideways and slumped listlessly beneath a gnarled old tree whose trunk was thick enough to offer some shade from the midday heat. The tree wasn't particularly large but it still had some leaves on it. Leaning back, Tina wondered absently if she would ever be able to get up from this place again. Without water, food or energy it seemed likely that this could be her final resting place. She slowly closed her eyes and pictured her mom at home, smiling at her. Tina smiled back, then reached out a small hand to touch her mom's face.

It was then that Tina Blanchette opened her eyes and made a simple discovery.

Lying back against the rough bark, she looked up to see swollen oranges on the end of several of the tree's branches. Blinking in disbelief, she got to her feet. Even then, the fruit remained above her. Panting and moving erratically, Tina clambered up the twisted old trunk until she reached the height of the lowest branches. She then lay on her belly and edged out along the thickest branch. When she reached the end, Tina reached out and pressed her small fingers into one of three oranges. Even as she made initial contact with the fruit, she could smell the sweet aroma from the waxy skin. Gripping the branch with her legs, she twisted three of the globes until they fell to the ground. Even though her stomach was cramping with hunger and thirst, Tina had enough self-control to reach for another laden branch and picked four more oranges, before she clambered back down from the tree.

After retrieving part of the broken beer bottle to use as a crude knife, Tina sat beneath the tree and began to feast on the finest fruit she had ever tasted. The juice ran down her chin like liquid gold as she guzzled chunk after chunk.

When she had finished, Tina climbed back among the branches and knocked down a further four oranges. She then lay back beneath the tree and closed her eyes. The combination of physical stress and emotional exhaustion was too much for the girl to cope with. For the first time in two days, her stomach felt relatively full, and she felt momentarily out of danger. It was only natural then that she fell asleep.

26

It was early evening and Leighton was moving around his kitchen, fixing dinner while Annie completed colouring in the outline of a castle. Leighton tipped the steaming mound of spaghetti from the colander into the white bowl. He then added three squirts of ketchup to create a smiling face and placed six circular slices of cucumber around the edge of the bowl like curls of strange green hair.

When the dish of food was placed on the table in front of Annie she giggled at the sight and slid her colouring book to one side. Leighton knew his creation wasn't the most nutritious dinner in the world, but at least his daughter would finish it. In any case she would soon be staying with her grandmother who would undoubtedly feed her more fresh vegetables than Leighton would.

After Annie was bathed and tucked up in bed, Leighton sat on a red and white spotted beanbag next to her bed. In the landing sat two carefully packed bags for her to take to her grandparent's house. One mainly contained clothes; the other – packed by Annie – was almost entirely full of soft toys.

As he completed the reading of *Little Red Riding Hood*, both Leighton and his daughter yawned. Leighton gently closed over the book and laid it on the small white bedside table. He then leaned over and kissed his daughter's forehead. By the time Leighton had levered himself up from the beanbag, his daughter's eyes were closed.

'I'm gonna miss you,' he whispered.

When he had stepped carefully to the doorway, Leighton was about to switch off the lights, when Annie spoke to him from the distant edge of sleep.

'Daddy...'

'What is it, honey?' Leighton remained in the doorway. Despite the fact that his daughter had spoken, her eyes remained closed. Leighton waited, knowing that she was already sliding down into those dark warm places.

'There aren't any real wolves around here, are there?'

'No, honey,' Leighton said, quietly, 'not around here anyway.'

Having closed his daughter's bedroom door, Leighton walked through to the living area of his home and slumped down on the sofa. Yawning, he dragged a hand over his face, and gazed around the room. The place was messier than it had been one Sunday when he had given the entire house a proper clean, but life with an eight-year-old and long working hours meant he could never fully keep on top of things. Still, if he could get through a couple of chores each night, then Sundays would be a little easier – then they could fit in some time getting ice cream at the beach and playing at the Tyson Street Park. But Leighton knew if he didn't force himself to get up, he would slide into sleep just as easily as Annie had done, only to wake up cold and painful a couple of hours later.

He got a fright as his attention was drawn to a clicking noise that came from the opposite corner of the room. He realised that the *Scooby-Doo* video cassette, which had still been running while the TV was off, had reached the end and then began to rewind. Whilst it hummed and clicked, Leighton picked up the remote from the sofa and switched the TV back on. Keeping the volume low, Leighton selected a local news channel, hoping to find a weather report. Unfortunately, he found himself looking at a grinning sports commentator.

He stood up and walked to the large window. In front of it, a drying rack was covered with Annie's washed clothes. Leighton dragged himself back to his feet and wandered over to the laundry. While his daughter slept, Leighton began to take each item off the airer, folded them and piled them neatly. He lifted off a couple of kindergarten T-shirts. They were white with a rainbow print on the front and Annie's name printed in puffy letters on the back. After folding them, Leighton turned back to the airer. Reaching out his hand, he picked up a pair of denim shorts. He began to fold them and then stopped. Staring down at the item of clothing, he frowned for a moment before gently placing them on the pile.

It was then that he glanced across at the TV, where a photograph of a small girl sat above the right-hand shoulder of the news anchor. The girl had mousy brown hair and was smiling directly down the lense of the camera.

Leighton walked, like a man in a trance, across the room towards the television. He crouched down and used the manual button to turn up the sound. He was eye level with the news anchor, listening intently.

'…who has now been missing for more than forty-eight hours? Police are appealing to anyone who may have been in the area at the time, to come forward. In other news…'

Leighton felt like he had been punched. Dragging a hand across his face, he stood up, then walked to where the telephone was hung on the wall just outside the kitchen.

Leighton picked up the handset and punched in the station number. He then held the phone to his ear and waited.

'Oceanside Police, how may I help you?'

Leighton recognised the voice. 'Lauren?'

'Yes.'

'It's Leighton Jones.'

'Hey, Jonesy.'

'Is Captain Levvy still around?'

'She was, hang on I'll check.'

There were a few moments of dead air whilst Leighton waited. Ellen Levvy – one of the station's five captains – was the head of Drug Enforcement and Missing Persons. Often the two areas were connected.

There was a click at the other end.

'Officer Jones, how may I help you?' The tone of voice was efficient and clipped.

'Hi, captain, I just wanted to pass on something about this missing kid they're talking about on the news.'

'Tina Blanchette?'

'Yeah.'

'Go on.'

'I just wanted to say that last night after I'd finished my shift, I drove home via Old Mill Way.'

'Bit out of the way,' Levvy said. It sounded like it might have been an accusation. Leighton was aware that Levvy knew of the time he had left the station without permission to check on Annie. In the weeks that followed that incident all of the captains in the station had viewed him with a mixture of suspicion and concern. He didn't want her thinking he had abandoned his post again.

'I was off duty at the time, captain.' Leighton said to clarify his position. 'I like the space out there – helps clear away the stresses of the day. Anyway, when I was driving through on the cut off along North Orchard Road a kid ran out in front of my car. It was a girl.'

'And?'

'Well, I reckon it could have been that kid.'

Leighton was almost sure he heard a sigh from the other end of the line.

'Okay, did you get a good look at this girl?'

'No, well not really. I slammed on the brake and she was gone.'

'Gone where?' the captain asked.

'Into the fields at the edge of the road. The grass grows high up there.'

'Was there anyone else around at the time – with you or any other vehicles on the road?'

'No, just me.'

'I take it you stopped. Did you get out of the vehicle?'

'Yeah and called out to her.'

'Did you get a response?' Levvy asked.

'No, she was gone in an instant.'

'Okay, officer, you know the routine – can you give me an approximate time of this sighting?'

'Around eighteen hundred hours.'

'And a description of the child?'

'Female Caucasian, approximately six or seven years of age, dressed in jean shorts and an orange or peach top. She crossed the carriageway from right to left when heading north.'

'Okay, Officer Jones, I've made a note of your sighting. Thanks for letting us know. I'll make sure that the details are passed on to the team working on the investigation.'

'Thanks, captain.'

'Enjoy the rest of your night.'

Having returned the phone handset to the cradle, Leighton walked back into the living area of his small home and sat down. Annie's fairy tale book remained near him on the sofa. Leighton glanced absently at the colourful picture on the front cover. It showed a girl in a red cape stepping blissfully through a deep forest whilst a sly looking wolf watched from behind a tree.

27

Tina woke up in the dark. She felt confused to no longer have the dry wood of the platform beneath her. Cold ground and a gnarled tree root pressed against her body. She was curled into a foetal position, frozen and stiff, but she could see a sprinkling of bright stars above some branches. They sparkled through the ghostly outline of the branches and offered Tina a sense of comfort.

Sitting up, she peered out at her desolate location. The light was just sufficient to see the pale landscape. The colourless dry ground, which seemed to stretch all around her in every direction looked like the surface of the moon.

As her teeth started to chatter, Tina knew that she couldn't stay out here all night but moving forward would mean wandering into the unknown. That was when Tina formulated a plan. She decided that she should return to the barn and collect another bottle of water. She vaguely remembered that a second one had been in the plastic tub beneath the faucet. But just as importantly, she also needed a piece of material to protect herself from the sun, and to serve as a blanket at night. If she couldn't find anything to use in the other buildings, she could perhaps use her piece of glass to cut a piece of the material in the barn.

She knew that if she made the journey at night then she wouldn't require any more fluids during the journey, and if she drank as much as she could from the faucet before setting off again, she would be able to retain the water in the bottle. Plus, if she had the oranges, she wouldn't be as thirsty. Her plan would allow her to travel much further, and if she had supplies, she might even make it home again.

So, having gathered up the fruit, she selected two of the softest feeling oranges and set off, limping through the starlit desert toward the barn.

Moving slowly through the warm night air, she focused on the shimmering heavens. At one point she saw a shooting star scorch the sky like a silent firework, and she made a silent wish to be back in her mother's arms, with the stranger unable to ever pursue them again. But her attention was taken up by the flashing lights of a passenger plane droning high above as it turned in away from her and on towards some distant place. Tina paused and tilted her small face towards the fading beacon of the plane. It reminded her of the one her dad had taken to Alaska. She remembered travelling home in the car after dropping him at the airport that night. Her mom had been crying for the entire journey home but was pretending she wasn't. She had been talking excitedly to Tina about Christmas and what kind of tree they might get, but Tina hadn't been listening. She had been secretly waving through her window at a passing plane in case that was the one her daddy was on.

When the lights of the plane had faded into the black sky, Tina wiped both her eyes then carried on her lonely journey.

***

It took Tina less time to return to the old buildings than she thought it would. At first, she could only see the humped silhouette of the hill blotting out the stars, but as the sky began to lighten Tina could discern the irregular shapes of the buildings as she neared them.

The first thing she did was run to the faucet and drink. She then fished out the remaining bottle and filled it up. She then carried it and her two oranges back inside the barn. As she stepped inside, the sun had almost fully risen, and shafts of light sliced through the thin gaps in the wooden walls.

Tina climbed back up on to the platform, only to sense the tiny bit of comfort it afforded her the night previously. She threw her two oranges up before securing her bottle and climbing back up on the hanging canvas belt.

Once she was secure in her location, Tina scurried like a small mammal to a distant corner where she settled back and, using her dirty nails, began to peel one of her oranges. She had only really uncurled one piece of skin when she heard the crunching sound of footsteps.

28

The waiting area of the Mind Space therapeutic centre was a rectangular room filled with diffuse light from a large opaque glass window. A white marble floor was dotted with comfortable chairs and a low coffee table, which was spread with a selection of glossy well-being magazines. Most of them featured smiling couples and hot air balloons. Leighton didn't touch any of them.

An hour earlier, he had kissed goodbye to Annie outside of his home as she climbed into her grandpa's white SUV. He hugged her tightly and told her to call if she needed anything, but he suspected that she would probably be too busy baking cookies and enjoying a break from school and her child-minder. As he watched the car slowly pull away from the sidewalk, he immediately wanted to run after it and say that he had changed his mind. But, despite being comforting, that wouldn't really help any of them. So, he had put on a brave face and smiled and waved as his daughter blew him kisses through the car window.

At the rear of the relaxing room, Leighton sat beside a glass water cooler. He stared at the small globe-shaped tropical fish tank on the opposite side of the rom. Leighton was absently watching some tiny metallic looking fish flit backwards and forwards in the illuminated water, when a door opened at the opposite room and the therapist – James Hernandez – leaned out.

'Good morning, Leighton, would you like to come through,' he said. It was not a question.

Leighton got reluctantly to his feet and crossed the waiting area.

The therapist held the door open for Leighton then closed it after he had entered the room.

'Hi, Leighton, have a seat.'

'Thanks,' Leighton said as sat in one of two chairs angled facing each other.

'So how have things been with you since last week's session – any better?' James asked.

'Yeah, things have been good,' Leighton said and looked at the floor.

'Really?' James asked.

'No, not great,' Leighton said with a shrug of his shoulders, 'but I'm still moving.'

'Not great in what way?'

'I don't know, I guess I sometimes feel like I'm barely holding it together. But Annie needs me so what does it matter, I should be strong.'

'*Should* is a dangerous word,' James said. 'It gives us impossible standards to measure ourselves against. It's only been, what, fourteen months?'

'Fifteen.' Leighton said.

'So, it's been less than a year and a half, and your job hardly provides you with much opportunity to relax, does it?'

'I don't need to relax,' Leighton said, firmly, whilst fixing his eyes on the window, 'I need to do my job and raise my kid.'

'Okay, well, in order to do both of them well, you need to relax. Have you been listening to the cassette I gave you?'

'Every day,' Leighton said, 'finding my calm place.'

'Does that work?' James asked.

'A little.'

'So how would you say you have you been, emotionally?'

There was a moment of silence, which was in itself a type of confession.

'Good.' Leighton said as he shifted in his seat and tried to sound upbeat. And it was true – at least in part. There were moments when he would take Annie down to the beach, and sitting in the warm fresh air he would feel almost good, almost like it had been before. But this was an occasional respite. Much of the time he felt mostly functional, and he would often remain in this mode until his kid was asleep, then he would climb into the shower cabinet and cry.

'You need to be honest with me,' James said. 'The process only works if you're willing to examine the truth.'

'Well,' Leighton shrugged, 'I suppose I have good days and not so good days – like most people, I guess.'

The therapist nodded. 'Thanks for being honest about that. It is perfectly normal to feel the way that you do. You do understand that, don't you?'

Leighton waited for a moment but finally nodded.

'But you should also know that some of your colleagues are concerned that you're still struggling to work through your loss. Is that a fair statement?'

'I suppose, but I might be *working through* it for the rest of my life. I don't think you just switch these things off.'

'No, you don't.' James said, softly. 'Tell me about the kid.'

'My daughter?'

'No, the other girl. Apparently, you've been talking about some kid you seen run in front of your car?'

'How do you know about that?' Leighton shifted in his seat.

'I get a daily update from the station at the end of shift. They fax it across. It's standard procedure in situations like this.'

'Wow.' Leighton rubbed at his temple in irritation. 'I didn't think I was such a liability.'

'It's not a matter of *liability*, Leighton; it's about your ability to cope effectively with the inevitable demands of the job.'

'I am able to do my job!' Leighton held his gaze.

'But you also reported seeing some child who may or may not be real.'

'She was real,' Leighton said, and looked out of the window where a couple of gulls where gliding in the blue sky.

'You may not know this, Leighton, but a vision of a child – like the one you experienced – can often represent a desire for lost innocence. You may have seen that girl as an expression of that, or perhaps as an outward vision of your responsibilities.'

'What does a *real* girl represent?' Leighton asked, defiantly.

After a pause, the therapist glanced down at his previous week's notes.

'How has Annie been doing over the last couple of weeks?'

'Okay.'

'Just okay?'

'Good,' Leighton corrected.

'No more bad dreams?'

'No,' Leighton said, 'that seems to have stopped.'

'That's good.'

'She's staying with Heather's parents for a couple of nights. We agreed to do it every six or seven months. We figured that it's a long drive down from Lancaster. So longer visits are better than more frequent ones.'

'That sounds like a good arrangement for everyone.'

'I just hope she sleeps okay there.' Leighton said, quietly.

'And what about your sleep, are you managing to get enough?'

'Yeah, mostly I guess.'

'But not always?'

'Sometimes I lie there thinking about what might've been, but I know that just screws my head up.'

'So how do you cope?'

'I switch the radio on and try to focus on the music instead of my thoughts.'

'What exactly are those thoughts?'

'That I'm a bad person,' Leighton said as if speaking to himself, 'that in the end I just let people down.'

'You can't be responsible for other people,' James said, softly.

'Yeah, well that's where we disagree,' Leighton said. 'I was responsible and I fucked up on my watch. And that failure hurt a whole lot of people – especially my kid, who never asked for any of this.' Leighton's voice cracked as he spoke. 'She goes to bed every goddamn night without a mom to brush her hair, or sing her songs. So now I will do what I can, for her and everyone else, because that's the least I can do.'

James glanced at his watch. 'Well, that's just about time up for this week. I think you're making real progress, Leighton. These are powerful realisations you are making.'

'All I need to hear is that I get to carry on being a cop for another week.'

'Well, it looks like you do.'

29

In the small front room of his bungalow, Len Wells was sitting in his easy chair, sipping bourbon while watching TV. He could abide most shows in the afternoon. Sometimes, if he was lucky, he would accidentally come across a football game or a quiz show but generally it was a toss-up between reruns of *The Waltons* or some crazy cartoon shows. On that afternoon, he had turned on to regional news – *Oceanside Today* – just in time to catch a special report on the spreading wildfires plaguing the state. However, there were so many repetitive images of red planes and burning hillsides that eventually Len lost interest and started to drift to sleep. He found it generally easier to sleep in the afternoon, when demons could be replaced by daylight and distractions.

When he awoke, Len found that the report on the wildfires had ended, and had been replaced by a fresh-faced woman who was cheerfully providing a recap of the day's top stories – including, of course, more about the fires. Len, who found the reporter's voice quite relaxing, let his eyes lazily drift closed again. In the slow fog of his thoughts he imagined slowly moving fire-planes dropping endlessly moving clouds of mist. His internal movie was accompanied by the voice of the woman speaking of fires, and a burst water pipe causing traffic problems on the Boulevard, and she also spoke of a spate of attempted break-ins down at the harbour – where midsized cruisers seemed to have been targeted. But when she eventually ended the headlines with an account of a seven-year-old girl missing from Fallbrook since Monday, Len's eyes shot open and his glass fell from his hand to smash on the tiled floor.

30

As she stepped through the glass doors of Oceanside Police Station, holding her daughter by the hand, Jackie Bucowiz sincerely believed she was doing the right thing. She had initially considered talking it through with Angela first, but she quickly decided that the woman had enough to deal with already. Jackie approached the reception desk where a young male officer was filling in a report. He looked up and smiled cheerfully.

'Good morning, how can I help?' he asked.

'I'm here about Tina Blanchette,' Jackie said, conspiratorially, 'I spoke to an officer called Drain on the telephone.'

'Do you possibly mean Officer Dane – from our missing person's team?'

'Yeah, that's it.' Jackie nodded. 'He asked me to come down in person.'

'Okay,' the officer said, 'if you'd like to take a seat for a moment, I'll see what I can do.'

Jackie led Suzy across the cool tiled floor to a row of red plastic chairs, which had been bolted to the floor in the corner of the reception area.

'Will this take a while?' Suzy asked as she climbed up on one of the chairs.

'I don't know, honey,' Jackie whispered. 'I hope not.'

'I'm hungry,' Suzy said in a tone that suggested she was possibly just bored.

Her mom unclipped her cream-coloured purse and reached inside. 'Here, honey.' She handed Suzy a small box of raisins.

'Can't we go to McDonalds?' Suzy asked.

'Sure, but after we speak to the police officer. This is important.'

'Mrs Bucowiz?'

Jackie looked up to see a tall officer standing in a doorway to the left of the reception desk.

'I'm Officer Dane, please come through.'

The woman and her daughter were led along a narrow corridor to a small room that contained a desk, four chairs and a potted plant in one corner. When all three of them were seated, Officer Dane removed a red plastic clipboard and a printed report sheet from a drawer in the desk. He pulled a pen from his shirt pocket and clicked the button on it.

'Okay, Mrs Bucowiz, you said on the telephone that you wanted to add something to you and your daughter's witness statements, is that correct?'

'Yes, I guess,' she said, sounding less than certain.

'So, I have it already recorded that your daughter had been playing with Tina Blanchette in an area of Fallbrook known locally as the creek, when they were approached by an unfamiliar adult male. Suzy left the scene to collect a toy from her home. She was gone for approximately ten minutes and, upon returning, she discovered that both Tina and the unknown male were gone. What is it you wanted to add?'

'Well, when I was asking Suzy about the man who she saw down at the creek I asked her if she'd ever seen him before.'

'Had you, Suzy?' Dane asked, turning his attention to Suzy who was absently eating her snack.

'Yeah,' she nodded, 'I think so.'

'And so I asked her all about it. Like how the guy spoke to Tina. Suzy said he was nice and friendly. But when she said he was wearing a baseball cap that got me thinking.'

'About what?' Dane frowned.

'About Tina's dad.'

'Go on,' Dane said.

'Well, we've only stayed in our current house for just under three years, before that we were up in Lakehead. So at the time David was around we only knew Angela's family in passing really. But even then, David was hardly ever home – he's one of those real outdoors guys who always seemed to be carrying a backpack to or from his jeep. Anyway, I just realised that I'd never seen him without a baseball cap on.'

'Well, a lot of guys wear them,' Dane said.

'Yeah, but when he left a couple of years ago Angela came round one night for the kids to play and for her to enjoy a couple of glasses of wine. With no husband on the scene, it just seemed like she could never get a night off. Anyway, once she was comfy, Angela told me that Dave had begged her to let him take Tina up to Alaska with him. That he kept calling regularly asking about it, but she kept hanging up on him. She said he was pretty much obsessed with wanting to see Tina again.'

'I see.' Officer Dane nodded sagely.

'I just… you know… thought, well, if this guy who wears a baseball hat, and who looks familiar shows up to abduct Tina, then maybe he could be her dad, right?'

'That would make sense,' Dane said. He then turned his attention to the child.

'Suzy, if I were to go next door and get a photograph of a man would you take a look at it for me?'

'Sure,' she nodded as she chewed on a raisin.

'Great.' Dane snapped his fingers. 'Excuse me for a moment, Mrs Bucowiz – I'll be right back.'

Officer Dane left the interview room, and, almost immediately, Suzy turned to her mom.

'When can we go?' she asked.

'After this,' Jackie said, 'it won't take much longer.'

Dane returned a moment later with a black and white print out of David Blanchette's driving license. He placed this on the desk in front of Suzy. The photograph on the copy was small and faint.

'Suzy,' Dane said, slowly, 'could this have been the man who spoke to you at the creek?'

'Think about it,' Jackie said, softly, 'try to remember.'

Suzy leaned over the paper, looked at the image for a moment and then, eager to go to McDonalds – where she might get a Happy Meal containing a brightly collared toy – nodded.

'Sure,' she said, 'that looks like the man.'

31

When Leighton left Mind Space centre, he ironically felt more stressed than he had before going in. James often told him that talking in therapy could raise some uncomfortable thoughts and feelings but in the end it would help. Leighton wasn't convinced.

Crossing the deserted parking lot, he realised that he needed to have a conversation with somebody back at the station.

As he drove across town, Leighton's thoughts kept drifting back to the small figure running across the road in front of his car. It seemed like a loop of movie reel playing round his head. For a moment he considered the possibility that James was correct – that the small figure was actually a construct of his stressed-out mind. After all, the kid had looked the same size, gender and build as Annie. But then again, the news report had confirmed that there actually was a real missing kid who matched the description. That couldn't be down to Leighton's emotional state.

Having parked at the rear of Oceanside Police Station, Leighton hurried through the glass doors and made his way to the administration section where he stopped outside a plain wooden door. He knocked and waited.

'Come in,' a female voice from the other side called.

Leighton opened the door and entered. He found Captain Levvy filing papers at her desk. She had set out four trays and a wastepaper basket was placed nearby.

'Officer Jones, can I help you?' she asked without stopping what she was doing.

'I've just come from my compulsory therapy session.'

'Ah, and how's that all working out for you?' Levvy asked with a tone of disinterest.

'The therapist asked me about the kid I saw on Old Mill Way on Monday.'

'What about it?' Levvy kept adjusting the papers.

'Captain, how did my therapist know about our conversation?'

'He gets updates.'

'But I only spoke to you last night. That means that the conversation about the kid would not have been on any update that had faxed across yesterday. The only way it would have been passed on would have been if you called in the morning without any agreed update protocol.'

'Okay.' Levvy shrugged, 'I told him – this morning on the telephone.'

'Why?'

'Well, I thought it might be linked to your stress.'

'Captain, I simply made a report of a sighting of a missing kid,' Leighton ran a hand through his hair, 'how the hell is that linked to stress?'

'Well you sound pretty stressed talking about it just now.'

'Has anyone looked into my sighting?' Leighton asked.

'Officer, you are an employee with some psychological issues, which have resulted in you abandoning your duties in this station. You gave a vague report that was unsubstantiated, of a child you saw eleven miles from where Tina was last seen. Miles – let me emphasise – not yards. I'm not sure what you expect anyone to do with that kind of information.'

'Has anyone looked into my sighting?' Leighton repeated.

Levvy sighed. 'The information you gave us was passed on to Officers Dane and Lorenzo, and if you attempt to second guess me again I'll have you up on a professional misconduct charge. Now, I imagine we both have work to do. Close the door on your way out.'

32

Tina peered, wide-eyed, through the gaps in the wooden barn wall. Her small heart was pounding in her chest, as she twisted her fingers together and stared straight ahead. In the isolation of such a desolate place, Tina felt the full extent of the danger represented by this scrawny man. The fact that he had returned was the most worrying thing for the small girl. Before now Tina had convinced herself that the stranger would probably forget all about her, and yet he had returned almost immediately. Fighting the urge to vomit – and lose what little food was in her stomach – Tina realised she needed to keep her eyes locked on the threat.

Leaning forward, she craned her trembling neck and placed her face against the wood. The spaces between the knotted planks were narrow but still wide enough to allow a glimpse of the courtyard. Outside, about thirty feet away where the flat ground merged with the tall grasses, the stranger was kneeling on the ground next to a large backpack. He appeared to be whistling cheerfully and was busy arranging something on the ground. Tina shuffled on her knees and shifted to get a clearer look. From her new location she discovered that the stranger was leaning forward and laying out a checked cloth on the dusty ground. Once it was flat he placed a rock in each of the four corners to weigh them down. He then turned round, grabbed the backpack and unclipped the top buckles.

After reaching inside the pack, the stranger pulled out various items: an orange tube of Pringles, a box of Twinkies, a packet of Oreos and two cans of Coke. Then, once the items had been freed he seemed to be considering each item in turn, picking them up and carefully arranging them like a shop display on the cloth.

At first, in the fog of her emotional confusion, Tina thought he was simply planning to have a picnic for himself. It was easy to imagine him sitting down on the blanket, perhaps with a napkin tied round his neck – shovelling food into his mouth to show Tina what she was missing. Then she realised with a dawning sense of horror that the food and drink was solely for her – to get her to come out from wherever she was hiding – like cheese in a mousetrap.

At one point, the stranger produced a tall glass from within the pack. He then picked up a Coke can and sparked it open with a loud hiss. She watched as the foaming soda ran over the stranger's hand like lava. He held it up to his mouth, and drank.

'Yummy!' he called out in a poor performance, 'that cola sure tastes sweet and cold.'

He then tilted the glass, half filled it with cola, then placed it back down on the cloth.

'I'll just leave some here in case anyone is thirsty!' he yelled.

Tina was vaguely aware of the saliva running down her small chin as she gazed in wonder.

Once he had finished arranging the various items on the checked cloth, the stranger stood up and dusted off his clothes. The way he looked down at the picnic suggested he was pleased with his work. He then shouldered his pack and walked towards the office, at which point he vanished from sight.

For a moment, Tina was worried that the stranger would come into the barn, but thankfully he didn't, and she figured that he must have gone somewhere else to watch and wait.

Even though she knew it was a trap, Tina had to force herself to look away from the pile of delights spread on the ground outside. She tried to remind herself of the story of *Hansel and Gretel*, and how sweets left out can lead to you being cooked and eaten. Yet the attraction was powerful. Sometimes she would glance at the picnic and especially the glass – she could imagine the countless bubbles floating to the surface.

In order to avoid the temptation of the picnic, she lay down and buried her face into the corner where the platform met the wooden wall. She closed her eyes and imagined she was home in her bedroom and that all of this was just a bad dream. In her mind, she could see her bedroom ceiling where the six glow-in-the-dark stars were stuck around the light – where her mom had stuck them when she was just a baby. She could imagine the feel of her favourite pink quilt, and she could recall the feeling of safety she got from being in her bedroom. Unwilling to leave such a pleasant place and return to reality, Tina slipped into a light sleep in which the boundary between reality and fantasy softened and blurred.

33

Angela Blanchette was standing in the doorway of her home when the police arrived. She hadn't slept or eaten in days. Instead she had set up a striped folding chair in her open doorway where she sat day and night – holding on to her daughter's pink blanket while praying for a miracle. The only concession she made at night was to close the screen door, but she was still there behind it, patiently waiting on her child to come back home.

When the car stopped, she recognised the two officers as the two who had visited her previously – Dane and Lorenzo.

She hurried down the path and met the two officers as they got out of the black vehicle.

'Have you found something?' she called over to them.

'No, sorry Mrs Blanchette.' Dane said as he and Lorenzo approached her. 'But if it's okay we'd actually like to speak to you about your husband?'

Angela was blindsided by the question. Didn't they realise David had been in Alaska for two years and was barely mentioned by anyone – including Tina. 'My husband, why?'

'We have been unable to contact Tina's father, we are considering the possibility that he is somehow involved in your daughter's disappearance.'

'What are you talking about?' Angela rubbed absently at her left temple.

'Mrs Blanchette, have you spoken to your husband in recent days at all?'

'No, but I've not spoken to him in months. He's in Alaska. I guess we don't communicate at all.'

'Yeah, we tried contacting him there, a local unit from Anchorage was dispatched to his home address without any luck.'

'I wouldn't say that would be all that unusual. He moved up there to be among the wilderness. He won't be sitting in the cabin waiting for folk to come visit.'

'Do you think your husband may be involved in Tina's abduction?' Lorenzo asked. 'Is that a possibility?'

'What?' Angela laughed in humourless way. The idea was ridiculous. 'No, of course not!' The expression on her face should have been enough to tell the officers how stupid the idea was, but they pursued it further.

'We'd like you to consider it.' Dane said, firmly. 'There are some pieces of corroborating evidence.'

'Are you shitting me?' Angela's raw emotion exploded from within her. 'Tina has been taken by some psycho and you're trying to suggest my ex-husband who is skipping about the mountains of Alaska trying to find himself is somehow involved? What do you think – that he drove three and half thousand miles to pick up his daughter – when he won't even pick up a damned telephone and speak to her? Yeah, good police work guys, real slick.'

'Calm down, Mrs Blanchette.' Dane said.

'You fucking calm down! Don't you think Suzy Bucowiz would have recognised my husband if he sat down to play dolls with her and Tina in the creek?'

The officers exchanged a nervous glance, and then the taller one spoke.

'We asked her if she recognised the man during her initial interview, she said she wasn't sure. However, when we showed her a photograph of your husband she confirmed that he might have been the person who had spoken with her and Tina at the creek.'

'What? No, this is insane.' Angela shook her head.

'Think about it, Mrs Blanchette. If it was your ex-husband who had taken Tina, that would possibly explain why he wanted rid of Suzy, and why Tina went willingly with him.'

'Get the hell out of here!' Angela said in a voice cracking with emotion. 'My daughter needs you to find her. She is not with my husband. God knows I wish he cared enough that he'd come back to see his daughter, but he doesn't. I told you already, get the hell out of here!'

The two officers reluctantly retreated to their car and climbed inside. As they drove away from Angela Blanchette she deliberately turned her back on them.

After the cops had gone, Angela sat back in her folding chair and quietly wept. For five years David had been her partner, her lover and everything. She knew that their life together hadn't been perfect, but nobody's was. But his anxiety had grown in him like a disease until he could no longer settle in his own home. He spent an increasing amount of time in the woods and mountains, but even that was not enough. He craved greater and greater freedom, and now at the time she needed him most, her husband was most certainly free.

In the months following his departure, there had simply been no phone calls or letters. He had simply left. At the time, he had promised that he needed a few weeks of space and time. After which he would definitely call. But that had been a hollow promise. Angela had been left to face the pain and humiliation but also the fact that he didn't seem to care about Tina. In order to conceal this, she had told friends that David often called asking to take Tina. She hated lying, but hated the reality more. That was why the claims of the cops were so ridiculous. David didn't even want to speak to his daughter, never mind abduct her.

34

In the small parking lot that faced on to the marina at Oceanside Beach, Leighton sat alone on the hood of his car. He was gazing beyond the various moored sailboats at the tumbling waves of the restless Pacific. Any time he came to the beach to clear his head, Leighton found the endless motion of the water more hypnotic and soothing than a thousand hours of relaxation cassettes. This was his safe space away from the politics of the job and the chaos of life. If it would pay his bills, he would happily swap his badge and gun for an apron and idle away his days serving coffees to tourists and fishermen at the harbour.

After his encounter with Captain Levvy, he had spent four long hours observing traffic on Highway 76, where he and Teddy had engaged in number of routine traffic stops, looking for uninsured vehicles and unsafe vehicles. They had found neither, something Leighton viewed as success, Teddy a failure.

At the end of their watch both men had happily gone their separate ways. Teddy had gone to his evening class in Criminology and Justice at Mira Costa College over on Barnard Drive; Leighton should've simply went home, but he still felt the stress of the day sitting on him like a backpack full of rocks. Returning back home would offer little respite either.

Annie had been away for just one night and already Leighton found the idea of stepping inside his silent house a bleak prospect. He hated silence. It reminded him that he was alone. That was why he had a small radio in every room of his house, and why he loved being near Oceanside harbour so much. Here it was impossible to escape the deep sound of the clashing waves, the call of the seabirds to each other and a constant stream of people fishing, surfing or simply relaxing. To Leighton, just being near the place was simply life-affirming, and he wished he could stay there for ever.

Closing his eyes, Leighton breathed in the fresh ocean air. He knew it was time to leave the harbour, but he still wasn't about to head home just yet. Something was calling him back to Old Mill Way. He doubted very much that Levvy had ever passed any information on to Dane and Lorenzo. That meant nobody was investigating the place he had suggested. Yet, if Leighton raised this issue with anybody it would only piss Levvy, Pierce and Winston off even more.

That meant it was up to Leighton to carry out his own investigation, regardless of the personal and professional risks.

***

Forty minutes later, Leighton turned off his engine and stepped out of his car. He had parked it in an area of scrubland on the edge of the road, hoping it wouldn't create an obstruction to passing traffic. He then made his way to the edge of the dusty road and began searching. Rustling through the dry grass, he peered around the edge of the road on both sides for a while, unsure of what he was even looking for.

Without any real strategy, he stepped deeper into the undergrowth, following the vague direction he believed Tina may have travelled in.

The ground Leighton was stepping through was uneven, dry and rocky, with little indication of a path. Tall tufts of dried grass merged with each other forming a golden labyrinth. After wandering north for half a mile or so, he stopped and gazed around at the rocky landscape. The girl could be anywhere, and a single cop wasn't going to do much good on his own. And that was assuming that the girl had ever been here, and Leighton wasn't quite as crazy as everyone seemed to believe.

Eventually, with a growing sense of defeat, Leighton turned and reluctantly began to make his way back towards the road. His journey through the wilderness was unsteady and at one point he felt her was drifting too far west.

Turning around by ninety degrees he made his way back towards the road. That was when he noticed the tiny piece of yellow plastic sticking out of the ground.

Crouching over the place where it lay, Leighton narrowed his eyes and peered at the tiny object, half buried in the dust. He recognised what it was straight away, because Annie had one at home just like it.

He gently pulled the plastic dog free and held it in his hand. It didn't look faded or cracked by months of exposure to the elements; it looked like it come straight from some kid's toy box to this place. There was no reason for this object to be out there in the middle of the dusty wilderness, unless a kid had recently taken it there.

35

Leighton got out of his car just as Dane and Lorenzo were leaving the station building in the direction of the car pool. He knew he would have to be quick to catch them before they got in their cruiser.

'Officers,' Leighton called over, 'have you got a minute?'

Both men stopped and turned. Dane – the taller of the two – turned to Lorenzo and said something that made him laugh. Leighton pretended he didn't notice and hurried across the parking lot to meet them.

'What's up?' Dane asked.

'You're the guys working the Blanchette case, aren't you?'

'That's right,' Lorenzo said. He folded his arms across his chest. 'What of it?'

'Did Levvy tell you that I made a possible sighting of the kid on Monday evening?'

The two officers glanced at each other for a moment. Then Dane nodded unconvincingly, 'Sure, she told us, of course.'

'So, have you guys been out to the location yet?' Leighton asked.

'No, not yet. It's on our list, though.'

'Good,' Leighton nodded with a grim smile. 'So answer me this, boys. What's the name of the location that's on your list?'

There was a moment of nervous laughter from Dane and Lorenzo.

'Come on.' Leighton continued pushing it, 'I mean you must know the actual name of the place, right?'

'Look, we're busy, man,' Dane said, 'I probably have it written down somewhere.'

'This is such bullshit,' Leighton said with real anger and frustration, 'Levvy didn't tell you, did she?'

'Jones,' Dane said with a shake of his head, 'stick to your own job. You have no business interfering with missing persons anyway.'

'Yeah?' Leighton said pointing his finger at the two officers, 'I guess that makes sense. You wouldn't want me getting in the way of your fucking inactivity.'

'What did you say?' Lorenzo tried to step toward Leighton in confrontation, but Dane held him back.

Leighton shook his head and walked away from Dane and Lorenzo. By the time they had reached their car, Leighton had already entered the station.

A young female officer who was working reception looked up when Leighton came in.

'Is Captain Levvy in?' Leighton asked, as he walked purposefully up to the desk.

'Hold on, I'll check.' the young officer said, as she picked up a telephone. However, he was stopped by another voice coming from the corridor to his right.

'That won't be necessary, Andrea,' Chief Winston said. 'Officer Jones, can I speak to you for a moment?'

Leighton followed the chief into his office where both men took a seat at opposite sides of the cheap wooden desk.

'What was that pissing contest in the parking lot all about?' Winston asked.

'Nothing,' Leighton said.

'Looked like something to me.'

Leighton sighed. 'I was just asking those two knuckleheads about the Blanchette case. That's all.'

Chief Winston closed his eyes in exasperation. When he opened them, he looked like a man who was rapidly running out of patience.

'Right, this ends now!' Winston said.

'What does?' Leighton asked.

'This missing kid madness you seem to be enjoying so much.'

'I wouldn't say I'm *enjoying* the fact that a kid could be out there with nobody looking for her.'

'I don't see what's so damned complicated about this. Ellen Levvy is in charge of missing persons, not you. You need to back off. Stop harassing your colleagues.'

'Why?' Leighton asked. 'What harm does it do to have another cop helping with the search?'

'Look, you've got no jurisdiction, it's not your case. You work traffic, period!'

Leighton listened and nodded politely, but his position remained unmoved.

'Sir, I just think the kid is still out there – alive, maybe.'

The older officer sighed and looked away for a moment. He then returned his attention to Leighton.

'Okay,' he said, soberly, 'you have a theory, and that's interesting. But what do you think would happen if we sent out a team to some godforsaken field every time a cop had a hunch?'

'It's not a hunch,' Leighton said, defiantly, 'I saw her, chief!'

'You saw somebody.'

'I saw Tina Blanchette!'

'Bullshit. The kid is most likely in Alaska with her dad.'

'Based on what?'

'Two credible sightings.'

'Credible my ass!'

'We have traffic officers to manage traffic – you are answerable to Captain Pierce. This case – and anything Captain Levvy or Dane and Lorenzo do – is not your concern. If you pursue it, I have to tell you – formally – that you will put your position as a serving officer at risk.'

'What does that mean, I'll be fired for trying to do my job?'

'Your *job* is dealing with highways and vehicles and drivers. If you stick to that we won't have a problem. Why don't you take the rest of the day, go pick up Annie and spend some time together?'

'I can't she's staying with Heather's folks for a few days – till Saturday.'

Winston looked at him.

'Jesus, Leighton, don't you think that's maybe part of the problem?'

'What do you mean?'

'Has she stayed with them before?'

'Once or twice,' Leighton said with a shrug.

'For as long as this?' Winston asked.

'No, not quite. But what difference does that make?'

'Well, don't you think that maybe you're projecting some of your mixed-up emotions on to this Blanchette case?'

'No, I don't,' Leighton said, but the fight was gone from his voice. Perhaps it was the thought of Annie sleeping somewhere else or the fact that no-one was prepared to listen, but he felt exhausted and defeated.

'Look,' Winston said, 'why don't you go get a coffee, freshen up your mind then get back to work. Maybe chase up some warrants, yeah?'

'Sure,' Leighton nodded.

36

Tina had been dozing – half curled in the angular corner of the roof – when she saw the figure. A narrow gap between the dried wooden slats of the barn wall allowed her a limited view of the open ground. She had only just opened her eyes when she initially saw a blur of colour pass by the gap.

At first, she thought the vision was just her imagination, some vision of hope conjured up by her desperate mind… but then she saw it a second time. Peering through the space between the colourless slats, Tina felt her breath jam momentarily in her chest.

A young man in a yellow T-shirt with a bright green backpack was hiking purposely through the dusty fields. Tina rubbed her eyes, wondering if she was dreaming. Yet the figure remained, striding through the bushes. He definitely wasn't the stranger either. This man was young and healthy. But a dark possibility sat on the fringes of Tina's thoughts – perhaps the stranger had sent him to lure her out. Yet that idea seemed unlikely. The young man didn't look like he was simply hanging around; he looked like he was on his way to somewhere else. All of these thoughts twisted in Tina's mind within a few seconds. Eventually, she conceded and realised that the fast-moving figure of the hiker probably represented her best and only chance of escape.

Tina cupped her hands to her mouth and tried to call out but her voice cracked and the noise was little more than a dry whisper. In desperation, Tina coughed and croaked, trying to form any kind of sound in her traitorous mouth. She tried a second time, and there was a dry croak. Finally, she grabbed at the brown beer bottle and held it to her mouth. Tilting the bottle upwards like a tiny bugler, Tina waited for what seemed like an eternity for the last two remaining drips of water to slide down on to her parched tongue. There was barely enough to swallow, but Tina tried. Letting the bottle fall away from her, she peered out at the figure and tried to call once more.

'Help!' Tina called from her rooftop prison. The word sounded muted and croaky in her dry throat, but at least it had escaped her mouth this time.

The hiker turned his head slightly, but continued walking. In a few seconds he would have vanished from her sight entirely. Tina shuffled stiffly on to her knees and put her face close to a wider gap in wooden slats of the wall and called again.

'Help! Up here!' she called. This time the sound was fuller and seemed to extend out from the building.

Despite Tina's apparent success. The figure continued moving sideways, sliding from her view.

'Help, over here!' she called again. This time her voice was louder, but by the time she had found her voice it was too late. The figure had vanished from sight.

Tina could barely believe it. With little emotional energy left, she pulled her knees to her chest and began to cry. Her throat felt hot and sore. She missed her mom and her home. But worse than that, she now realised that it was quite likely she would see neither of these ever again. And then, through the blur of tears, she saw a flash of bright green reappear through the gap in the wall. Wiping the tears from her eyes, Tina gasped and felt her heart rate suddenly increase.

Pushing her face back to the gap she saw him again – clearly now.

The hiker had returned and was standing looking pensively toward the buildings. He held a hand up to his eyes to shield them from the sun and was peering directly at her. Then he glanced down at the checked cloth in front of the building and frowned.

'Hello?' he called. 'Is there somebody there?' The expression on his face suggested that he was unconvinced he had actually heard anything at all.

Tina smiled and a sense of relief washed over her. The hiker was taking a small pair of binoculars from his pocket. That meant he could possibly see her if she waved.

She was just about to call out to him again when she saw the stranger silently rise out of the rippling grass behind the hiker. He looked like some monstrous snake emerging from its lair. Tina tried desperately to scream out a warning, but her open mouth only croaked once more. She watched in horror as the stranger grabbed the hiker around the neck and pulled him down into the dry grass.

Tina couldn't see what was happening, except for an occasional leg kicking at the air.

She hoped desperately that the hiker was strong enough to fight off the stranger, and that he would be the one to emerge from the struggle.

Eventually, the stranger stood up from the disturbed grass. His face was shiny with sweat and his lower lip was bleeding, but he was grinning. He looked towards the buildings, clearly unsure of which one she had called from.

'I know you're there!' the stranger called. His voice sounded deep and hoarse. Tina could see that his hands were trembling. 'I had to do that, he was going to hurt you! He was one of the bad people who had come looking for you. And there will be more of them coming after him, too. They'll be wondering why he hasn't returned with any information. Then they'll come for you.'

After he finished speaking, the stranger moved his head from side to side, carefully scanning the area for any sign of the girl. Seeing no movement, he carried on shouting to nowhere in particular.

'It's not too late for you. If you come out now, there's still a chance that we can go get you some food and water, then meet up with your mom. She's waiting and she misses you something awful. But I'm trying to keep you both safe, and all the time that I'm spending out here looking for you means that she's not safe.'

He paused for a moment then wiped the back of his neck. 'So really, if anything happens to her, I guess it'll be your fault.'

Tina knew he was lying but the words still hurt just the same. Her small lips trembled and she started to cry.

Through the blur of her tears, she watched as the stranger picked up the hiker's feet and began to drag him from where he lay into the shadows of the trees.

37

Leighton was sitting on the back step of the fire exit of Oceanside Police Station. He had jammed the door open and was sitting with his back to the empty recreation room. Scattered around his feet were hundreds of crushed cigarette butts. He was holding a polystyrene cup of coffee, and was lost in memories of the previous November when he and Annie had gone to the Carlsbad Village Fair, where she had spent almost an hour leaping joyfully around in the bounce house before they had feasted on pancakes soaked in melted chocolate, washed down with homemade root beer. Annie had said it was the best food she'd ever tasted and asked if they could go back every weekend. When Leighton explained that it was an annual event, she had looked at him with genuine sadness in her eyes.

'I don't understand why the good things can't last for always,' she had said.

Leighton told her that he didn't understand either, then he hugged her.

***

He took a sip of coffee and then glanced down at the pile of white envelopes stacked in his lap. He was starting to plan which was the best route to drive, when he was distracted by the arrival of an unfamiliar female officer in the room behind him. She appeared to be struggling to operate one of the two recently installed hot drinks vending machines. She pressed the coffee button several times in increasing frustration. Leighton turned fully around.

'You okay there, miss?' he called over to her.

The woman stopped pressing random buttons and turned toward Leighton. 'Sorry, I just can't seem to get this thing to work.'

'Don't worry, it's not your fault,' Leighton said with a smile, 'the coffee button on that one never seems to work properly, but if you just select *latte* it should work fine.'

As she followed Leighton's advice, the young woman looked genuinely surprised when the temperamental machine gurgled to life and began dispensing her steaming drink.

'Thanks,' she said as she removed the hot drink from the tray. 'Is it okay if I join you out there?'

'Sure,' Leighton nodded and shifted over on the step.

'I'm Lisa,' the other officer said as she sat down on the step next to him.

'Leighton Jones – traffic. So, are you just starting with us?' Leighton asked.

'Yep, just started this week as a dispatch operator.'

'You a rookie?'

'No,' she said with an expression of mock indignation, 'I've done four years already, just got transferred down here from San Bernardino.'

'Transferred, huh? What did you do?' Leighton sounded intrigued.

'I guess I didn't really see eye to eye with my captain.'

'You don't get transferred for that.' Leighton chuckled. 'Otherwise I'd be working somewhere on the east coast, or Europe even.'

'You do if you threaten them,' Lisa said.

'Oh.' Leighton raised his eyebrows. 'That'll do it.'

'Yep, so me, my husband and my babies had to up sticks and move to here, thanks to my big mouth.'

'Well, I suppose there are worse places to end up,' Leighton shrugged. 'The beach down at the pier is nice for kids. You got a couple then?'

'Yeah, for my sins,' Lisa laughed.

'How many you got?' Leighton asked.

'Two boys – three if you count my husband. The smallest is only three, his big brother is six.'

'Can't be easy leaving them,' Leighton said, knowingly.

'No, but it pays the bills,' Lisa shrugged. 'How many have you got?'

'Just one – my daughter. So how you finding the job working dispatch?'

'Yeah, fairly good.' Lisa took a sip from her cup. 'Not exactly the most exciting first week. A couple of drugs busts, and a missing kid.'

'They still haven't found her then?' Leighton sounded concerned.

'Nope, her mom calls every few hours for an update too. Poor woman must be hurting pretty bad.'

'What's the story with it? Nobody seems to be saying much.' Leighton tried to sound casual.

'Not much,' Lisa said, 'a team were dispatched to the last known location and interviewed the witnesses. Apparently the girl was playing with a friend near her house when she vanished. It's a case of she's a single mom, absent father has been gone for a years or so. Kid may be a runaway – in any case the woman must be going through hell. I hate the ones with kids the most.'

'Me too,' Leighton sounded casual, but he had already decided that there was somebody he probably needed to speak to, if only to gain approval.

He drained the last of his coffee, then stood up.

'Listen, it was nice to meet you, Lisa. I best be moving. I've got a bunch of DUIs who need to be notified of a change to next week's driver awareness class. I don't want them showing up at the wrong place then getting hit with a bunch of warrants for non-attendance. You take it easy, especially on those night shifts.'

'I will,' she said.

After the older officer had left, Lisa Martinez finished her coffee and considered her encounter. Leighton seemed nice enough; friendly and not as arrogant as some of the more experienced cops she had encountered. She therefore wondered why the first person she had met that morning – Teddy Leach – had told her to stay clear of him. When she had asked why, Teddy had said because he was on his way out of Oceanside P.D.

38

When Leighton pulled up in his car on the street outside the Blanchette home, the blonde-haired woman who had been sitting on a plastic lawn chair on the porch of the house stood up. Holding up her hand to shield her eyes, she peered expectantly at the unfamiliar red car.

In the hour previous to that, Leighton had quickly delivered six letters notifying the convicted individuals of a change of venue for their scheduled DUI classes to various addresses around the city. His efficiency meant that he had created some free time to visit Fallbrook without appearing to be neglecting his traffic duties.

The Blanchette house looked tired, as if it, too, was feeling the heat of the day – or perhaps the weight of the emotional situation. Leighton knew that the cool ocean breeze rarely reached this far inland where the city started to fade into the sweltering countryside. Whilst a house out in Fallbrook may have seemed like an attractive option in winter, the rest of the year was too hot to bear. This made property in the area at least a third cheaper than the city.

As he got out of the car, Leighton took out his badge and walked along the hot gravel path toward the woman.

'Mrs Blanchette?' he asked as he narrowed his eyes against the glare.

The woman nodded, but only her head moved – as if the rest of her was momentarily frozen.

'My name is Leighton Jones; I'm a police officer. Can I speak to you for a couple of moments?'

Leighton noticed absently that in one of her hands the woman was holding a small crushed ball of pink fabric. Initially, he thought it might be a flannel but a splash of colour suggested it was a small

T-shirt. He figured that it was probably the one Tina had been wearing the day before she vanished and still smelled of her.

'Has something happened, have you found her?' Angela Blanchette asked. For a moment, the woman's grey eyes lit up with a visible sense of hope.

'No, I'm sorry,' Leighton said, 'not as far as I know.'

'Oh.' Angela Blanchette sighed and lowered herself back down into the chair. Her fingers twisted together with the knot of fabric locked in her hands.

'Look.' Leighton rubbed the back of his neck with one hand. 'I want to be honest with you, Mrs Blanchette. I'm not out here as part of the official investigation. I guess I'm here unofficially.'

'What?' Angela Blanchette frowned. 'I don't understand. You're not part of the investigation?'

Leighton crouched down to meet her eyes. 'I'm just a traffic cop, but I wanted to ask you a few questions.'

'Why? This has nothing to do with traffic.'

'You're right.' Leighton nodded. 'I'm just not convinced that my colleagues have been looking for Tina in the right place.'

'What?' Angela Blanchette frowned. 'They told me they were following evidence. Why wouldn't they be looking in the right place?'

'Look, this is just my own personal view. I'm no expert. Like I said, I just work traffic, nothing else, but I think I could help.'

'Mr, with all due respect, my daughter is missing, I don't care you're a goddamn circus clown, if you know something that could help, tell me!'

Leighton took a deep breath, then crouched down so that his eyes were level with Angela's.

'On the day your daughter vanished, I was driving home from work and I saw a kid who looked like Tina.'

'Where?' Angela looked as if someone had just thrown a bucket of water over her.

'Out by Old Mill Way. I was driving back from work and a girl just ran across the road right in front of me. Would Tina ever have been out in that area of the city before?'

'No, she's seven years old for God's sake. Have you told the other cops about this?'

'Yeah,' Leighton shrugged his shoulders, but they think that I was mistaken and it couldn't be her.'

'So, nobody has checked this place out?'

'I have spent a few hours out there, and I'm going back out there again this afternoon.'

'Did you find anything?'

'Just this.' Leighton reached into his pocket and produced the small plastic dog. He carefully held it out for the woman to inspect. 'Does it look familiar?'

'I guess. She has a tub full of these sorts of things in her bedroom.'

'I just thought that if she had been playing with dolls when she vanished…'

Angela sighed, and it sounded like it came from her soul. 'Everybody has a theory. The cops are trying to say that my ex-husband might have taken her up to Alaska. My sister thinks she's possibly being held for ransom. I even got a telephone call from a wacko psychic late last night telling me that Tina had been abducted by a bus full of killers. The psychic said they could give me a little more information but only for a hundred bucks.'

'Parasites,' Leighton said.

'So, I have to ask – what exactly is it you want from me? I've got nothing left.'

'I Just want your permission to look for Tina in the place I saw her. Everybody thinks that I'm out of line, but I want to do this. I just don't want to interfere, or for you to think I'm messing with things.'

'Do the other cops know what you're doing?'

'Yeah, but my boss has pretty much told me to leave the case alone.'

'So why do you even care?' Angela asked.

'I have a daughter – Annie – the same age as Tina. I know how I would feel if she was out there and nobody was looking in the right place.'

'Look, forgive me for not believing that you're onto something. But I don't care what oddball theories you have, Mr Jones. If you can do anything that could help find her I'd appreciate it.'

'Thank you.' Leighton nodded. 'I will. Listen, is there somebody here with you? Somebody who can support you?'

Angela shook her head. 'There was once, but he's gone. My parents are both dead, and I have a sister who lives on the other side of the country. But I'll be okay if I can just get my daughter back.'

'Then I'll get on to it,' Leighton said with small self-conscious smile.

He turned to go but Angela Blanchette wasn't quite finished with him.

'Can I ask you something – and I want you to be honest with me? Nobody else seems to be.'

'Sure,' Leighton shrugged.

'How much experience do you have as a cop?'

'Nineteen years.'

'Do you think my daughter is still alive?'

'Yes,' Leighton said, softly, 'I think she might be.'

'Then you get the hell out of here and go to wherever you think my baby might be.' Leighton nodded and felt a renewed sense of purpose. He recognised the pain in this woman's eyes – it was the same as the one he often saw in the mirror.

'I'll let you know if I find anything,' Leighton said as he turned to go. 'Don't lose hope, Mrs Blanchette.'

'Angela,' she said, softly.

'Okay, Angela. I'll be in touch,' Leighton said as walked to his car with a renewed sense of purpose.

'Hang on!'

He had almost reached the car when she called after him, and then came running barefoot along the path to the car. She came up to Leighton and handed him a small yellow note. 'It's my phone number.' As she passed the note she gripped Leighton's hand. 'Thank you for doing this,' she said, and then let him go.

39

The arm of the hiker snagged on a tree root. The stranger had to pull on his legs even harder to free it. He grunted with the effort, which was intensified by the scorching sun. Dragging the body through the sparse woods wasn't easy, but it was necessary. He was hoping to find a place to conceal it.

Although the deserted old farm wasn't likely to be visited soon, the fact that the hiker had not been holding a map or compass suggested that he knew the route, and if he knew it then maybe others did too. That raised a more alarming possibility for the stranger – that the hiker wasn't alone. These walkers travelled in little clusters. Perhaps this one had been with others who would then show up half an hour later, looking for their friend at the agreed meeting place – such as the faucet on the old farm. If they found a body, the cops would arrive, and the hidden girl would go to them. He couldn't let that happen.

The other concern would be that any passing helicopters looking for a missing child, might just notice a dead guy lying in the grass – then the previous scenario would play again.

That was why he had to get the body out of there.

Then he would have to get out the area for a little while. If the kid saw the attack, she wouldn't be going anywhere for a while. Either she would view the rest of the world as dangerous, or she would view him as dangerous; both of these would keep her cowering in the shadows until he returned.

40

After driving south east for an hour, Leighton left the highway, taking the exit for Old Mill Way. As he passed by the various homes dotted across the landscape he glanced at them and wondered about the lives of their inhabitants. He stared at one place where a young woman was sitting on the steps drinking a beer, whilst a young man in shorts painted the eaves of their home. Leighton quietly envied them – starting out in life together, enjoying the excitement of creating their nest. He hoped they could make it last.

The afternoon was hot and the AC unit was struggling to keep the temperature bearable.

After what seemed like an eternity, Leighton finally pulled up on the edge of the road where he had first seen Tina. It seemed like that sighting had been weeks earlier not just days.

Climbing out of the car, he reached into the back and pulled out a small black rucksack, which he tossed over his shoulder and then locked up the vehicle. He gazed around for a moment, feeling that time was somehow folding back on itself. The quality of air, the temperature and the sound of the insects, was eerily familiar. It almost seemed possible that, if he waited there long enough, time would shift and a small girl in an orange T-shirt would burst from the grass and race across the road before vanishing on the other side.

Of course that was just a fantasy. If time could be reversed, he would find a way to go back into his past and make things somehow right again.

He shook this thought from his mind and stepped from the road into the sea of dry grass. As he left the road behind him, Leighton felt increasingly pessimistic about the scale of the landscape in front. But he had a promise to keep to Angela Blanchette, and so he kept on moving through the long grass.

***

By 2pm Leighton had wandered around the site for almost an hour. Occasionally, he became excited when he found what appeared to be a track, only to find it to vanish after only ten or twenty feet.

He stopped once or twice and used a pair of old field binoculars to survey the area. The ground was tough, and Leighton figured it would be near impossible for a kid to cross on foot. Leighton estimated that the easiest route the young girl could have taken would to be south-west. The landscape ran on a downward elevation and would have looked like it was leading to the ocean, which was about ten miles away. The ground on either side was much higher, meaning Tina could be in one long, narrow valley. That may have provided her a sense of security as she hurried away from danger. It would be impossible to search on foot, but a sweep from the air would easily cover such a definite route.

***

When he finally emerged from the grass back at the location of his car, Leighton found a large camper van was parked next to his vehicle on the edge of the road. An elderly couple were sitting in the front seats, peering at a map. They both glanced up in surprise at the dusty police officer emerging from the long stalks of grass. The man wearing a white cap leaned out of his open window and called across to Leighton.

'Is everything okay, officer?' He waved a hand, gesturing toward the field.

'Yeah, everything's fine.' Leighton called back, but he kept on moving.

When he reached his car, he unlocked the door and climbed inside. He had only taken a couple of deep breaths when he was startled by a knocking on his driver-side window. He turned to find the man from the camper standing by his car. Leighton sighed and rolled down his window.

'May I help you, sir?'

'What was going on in the field?' the old man asked.

'Nothing,' Leighton said, 'I was taking a pee. That's all.'

'With a backpack, I don't think so. I think we have a right to know.'

'Sir, you can think whatever you want,' Leighton said and, having started the engine, drove off.

***

Returning back to his small house, Leighton felt both physically and emotionally exhausted. The house was cold and without Annie in it the place seemed like an empty shell. He wandered through to the kitchen and made himself a microwave meal. Whilst it was humming away in the kitchen, Leighton walked to the phone and picked it up. He dialled his mother-in-law's number, held the handset to his ear, waited. It rang a couple of times then switched automatically to voicemail.

'Hey, it's Leighton, just checking in with my baby. Hope you're having fun, pumpkin. I'm looking forward to see you on Saturday. Love you, dad.'

After replacing the handset, he walked into Annie's room where a selection of brightly coloured, wide-eyed toys gazed at him from the bed. After wandering over to it, he slowly sat on the small mattress and picked up the purple pillow printed with pink clouds. Holding the fabric to his face, he breathed in the faint scent of his daughter's watermelon shampoo. If he closed his eyes, he could imagine she was sitting there beside him.

'I miss you,' he said to the empty space, his voice sounding small and quiet.

Eventually, he slumped forward on his daughter's empty bed and wept. Leighton's head was facing downwards and hot tears ran down his nose to splash on the tiled floor.

'I miss you so much,' he said to the air.

41

Tina had remained crouched on the small wooden platform of the barn for hours. The sudden killing of the hiker had left her petrified, but now, as the sky darkened, she had come to the realisation that remaining in this part of the building was perhaps even more dangerous than being out in the open. The stranger certainly knew that she was somewhere in the area. It would therefore only be a matter of time before he eventually found her.

In her increasingly exhausted state, it seemed likely that he could easily creep up on Tina while she was sleeping on that small ledge. And yet, if she tried to leave the barn the stranger might still be in the area, hidden like some overgrown spider ready to pounce at the first sign of movement. At least in the open she had a chance of hiding among the trees and bushes.

Consequently, Tina made her escape from the barn incrementally. Having silently lowered herself down from the raised platform she stood at the edge of the deep pit and listened. There was nothing but the sound of insects chatting to each other in the fading light. But the silence was not enough to reassure Tina; she was wary of how silent and patient the stranger could be.

After ten minutes, Tina found enough confidence to creep to the doorway of the barn and looked out at the crumpled checked cloth and scattered packets of food. Her shrunken stomach rumbled at the sight of the packet of Oreos, but she forced her eyes to look away. That was a trap, and she wouldn't let herself be drawn toward it. Instead, she crept back over to the huge pit in the floor of the barn. The sunken machinery looked large and dangerous, but perhaps it might help her. A metal ladder bolted to the side of the pit wall led down twelve feet into the cavity where the two machines sat. The larger one reminded Tina of the one they used to empty her school swimming pool but that was much newer and safer looking than the one in the pit. The smaller machine looked unfamiliar. Both machines were jagged and rusty.

Tina gazed into the sunken shadows. She knew if she could get the stranger to go down into the pit, she would have a greater chance of escape. While he was down in that space, he would be unable to see where she was. That made climbing back up the hill and returning the way she had first come less of a risk.

After creeping outside, she approached the site of the mock picnic. Glancing carefully around, she grabbed the tube of Pringles and then ran back into the barn. Once inside, she tore the lid off the tube and began frantically cramming the potato chips into her mouth. They tasted strong and dry, but Tina didn't care. Her body badly needed the salt and carbohydrates. She then replaced the lid and dropped the tub into the pit. It hit the bottom of the cavity and bounced into one corner. But Tina was worried that the tube alone would not be enough to catch the stranger's attention.

She thought for a moment, before deciding she had to make a necessary sacrifice.

Taking off her one remaining sandal, she dropped it into the pit too. It landed a couple of inches away from the tub. Hopefully, the stranger would notice them and climb down into the pit. Then she could run off in any direction she wanted because he wouldn't be able to see from down there.

Having completed her plan, Tina decided she needed to find somewhere new to hide and wait, but she was too afraid to venture out of the barn again until it got fully dark, so she found a corner near the rear open doorway and crouched barefoot in the shadows.

42

While Tina crept like a thief around the ruined farm, the stranger was fifteen miles away. He had just pulled into the public parking lot of the Pilot 1497 Piper Ranch Road Truck Station. Not far away from where he sat, a couple of long-distance trucks were parked together like sleeping beasts, whilst a third one was filling up with fuel from the oversized gas pumps.

On the passenger seat of his car a newspaper was folded over to reveal a small article on the disappearance of Tina Blanchette. The stranger had initially read it simply for pleasure, and the resulting sense of power it gave him to know he was affecting the world. However, things changed when he read one particular line in the article. It offered him an easy way to guide the police off the trail for good… *police are also looking into the possibility that the girl may have been taken by her father to his home in Alaska.*

He got out of the car and began pacing backward and forward; rehearsing different accents.

After wandering around the lot for a few moments, the stranger walked toward the payphone outside the restrooms and picked up the handset. He pulled a crumpled scrap of paper from his pocket, dialled the number that was scrawled across it, and waited.

'Hello, Oceanside Police – how may we help?'

'Hey there,' the stranger said in a southern accent. 'My name is Maurice Enfield. I work hauling logs from Calgary… Listen, it might be nothing but I reckon I saw that little girl, the one who was on the news.'

'One moment, please.' There was a quiet buzz from the handset as the call was transferred.

'Hello.' It was a different voice this time. 'This is Officer Dane of missing persons. Do you have some information regarding the Blanchette case?'

'Yes, sir, I guess I do.' The stranger attempted to sound casual, 'Look I don't want no reward or that kind of thing. I just wanted to let you know that I think I might've seen that kid.'

'When and where was this?' Dane asked.

'It must've been Wednesday afternoon, on the northern side of the Alaskan border. I stopped off at a gas station on Dempster Highway junction Klondike Highway in the Yukon Territory. They have this little area in the shop with a couple of coffee machines and a sandwich counter. Nothing fancy, but enough to perk you up on the longer routes.'

'And this was where you think you saw somebody resembling Tina Blanchette?'

'Yeah, I reckon it was her alright. She was sitting with some guy – seemed real comfortable with him too. He was in front of me getting the kid a hot chocolate. I heard her say that she missed her momma, but he told her not to worry.'

'Can you describe what the girl was wearing?'

'Sure. She was dressed like they said on the TV, except she was wearing a hooded top. It was red and looked kinda new. She called the guy 'dad' couple times, I remember hearing that. Oh, and she had one of those kiddy tattoos on the back of her hand – the kind you lick and stick on.'

'Can you remember what it looked like?' the officer asked.

'Let me think…' He paused for emphasis. 'Oh yeah, it was a kind of fairy – like from a fairy tale or one of those Disney movies.'

'Can you describe the man who was with her?'

'Not really, bud. He was in front of me mostly and didn't turn around. Now that I think about it, maybe he didn't want to be seen. Seemed average build, brownish hair. And like I said, he seemed to get on well with that kid.'

'Thank you Mr Enfield. Can you give me a number we can reach you on?'

'Sure, but it'll have to be my work phone – I spend all my time on the road so my home number would be pretty useless.'

'A work number is fine,' the officer said.

The stranger hung up the phone after relaying a false number, then casually walked back to his car. If they traced the number he rang from, it would be a truck station, which would make it seem a little more convincing.

He felt confident his performance would be good enough to keep the cops busy for a while, allowing him to carry on in the morning undisturbed.

43

When he arrived at the police station, Leighton walked through to the dimly lit locker area. He was hoping to pick up the keys to the Explorer and get to work quickly – that way he might be able to build in another drive to Old Mill Way. However, as he was about to turn the key in his metal locker door, Leighton was approached by a small middle-aged officer named Tony Evans.

'Hey, Jonesy,' he said. 'The chief asked me to catch you and tell you to pay a visit to his office.'

'At this time in the morning, any idea what about?' Leighton asked.

'Nope, just left a note at reception to catch you when you arrived.'

'Sounds like I'm in the shit,' Leighton said as he pocketed his key.

The other officer, who was already walking away, turned back and offered a wry smile. 'Jonesy, cops like us live in a sea of shit. But a visit to the chief just means the shit is getting so deep that it's getting on the shoes of the people at the top – and they don't like that. Just remember to smile and nod, amigo.'

'Thanks for the advice, Tony,' Leighton said and walked back through the building.

Eventually, the scuffed flooring beneath his feet gave way to carpet as he entered the management area of the station. The entire area smelled of cheap coffee and furniture polish. The chief's office was at the very end, flanked on either side by four smaller rooms for each of the station's captains. Their office doors all had semi-transparent windows; the chief's did not. This created an intimidating impression, but Leighton wasn't too worried – Chief Winston had always played fair with him.

Leighton knocked on the plain wooden door and waited. When his captain opened it, he could see further into the room where the chief was sitting at his oak desk.

He glanced up at Leighton. 'Come in, officer,' he said.

As he walked into the office, Leighton heard the door close behind him. He had assumed the captain had left, but he turned around and was surprised to find Pierce was still in the room.

'You sitting in on this?' Leighton asked.

'Take a seat, Jones,' he said with an air of indifference.

Both men waited until Leighton had sat at the desk before continuing.

'I expect you know why we have asked to see you?' Chief Winston asked.

'Well.' Leighton shifted uncomfortably in his chair. 'I didn't think it was to discuss the Super Bowl.'

'Lose the attitude, Jones,' Captain Pierce said. 'This is a formal disciplinary meeting.'

'Disciplinary? For what?' Leighton struggled to conceal his anger.

'For the hours you are wasting chasing some imaginary kid. We got a call from a concerned member of the public who said that there was a confused looking guy dressed as a cop wandering around the countryside over at Old Mill Way. They thought the cop was there as part of an official investigation, and the cop they spoke to was arrogant and rude.'

'Could've been anyone,' Leighton said as he gazed at his feet, waiting for the shit-storm to pass.

'The plates of the vehicle parked in the area matched your car.' Pierce said, happily.

Leighton sighed. There was nothing he could say. Pierce was head of traffic and would have checked the plates in seconds. 'Well, I guess I was probably taking a walk, getting some air at the end of my shift.'

'Bullshit!' Pierce spat the word out.

'Okay, what do you want to hear? Yes, it was me. Yes, I was using my own time to help search for a missing little girl, in the hope that it might do some good. Case closed.'

'Jesus Christ,' Winston said as he shook his head. 'I don't understand why you are deliberately pursuing this.'

Leighton suddenly felt his frustration bubble up, but he fixed his attention on the floor.

'I don't understand why the department isn't. Isn't it our job to follow every lead to exclude it from an investigation? It seems like we exclude *before* we investigate.'

'You're out of line, officer!' Winston said and pointed a stubby finger at Leighton.

Leighton glanced up from the floor and looked first at the chief then the captain's face.

'With all due respect, sir, I can't see that I'm doing anything wrong.'

'Teddy Leach would disagree,' Pierce said with a wry smile.

'I don't care about that rookie,' the chief said, 'I do care about the fact you are interfering with Captain Levvy's live investigation.'

'Investigation?' Leighton laughed. 'I wish to hell there was an investigation. Who is out there looking for the kid?'

'There are officers on the case right now.' Winston said.

'Okay, maybe. But none of them are looking in the right place. There is a valley running south from where I saw the kid. It runs from Old Mill Way down to the coast for a few miles. All it would take is a helicopter crew to sweep it.'

'All it would take?' Pierce said, 'Are you going to pay for the aviation fuel?'

'If I have to.'

'Fuck off!' Pierce said.

The chief shot him a glance that suggested he needed to keep this professional.

'Officer Jones, this is the last discussion we are going have about the Blanchette girl. Any further efforts you make to investigate this matter will be considered professional misconduct. Do you understand?'

Leighton looked at his chief. He could barely believe that his commanding officer was suggesting that looking for a missing kid was somehow a bad thing for a police officer to do.

'Do you understand, Officer Jones?' Winston repeated.

'Yes, sir,' Leighton replied. He understood it perfectly. That did not, however, mean that it would in any way deter him from looking for Tina.

'Can I go start my shift now?' Leighton asked, trying to remain professional. 'I should have clocked in twenty minutes ago and I don't want Teddy Leach having to report me for late-coming.'

'You don't need to stress about that,' Pierce said, 'I have already sent Tim Miller out with Teddy today. That'll give you both a break. You're on paperwork for the remainder of the week.'

'And just to confirm,' Pierce added, 'that means you do not leave this station.'

'Are you serious? Is this some type of punishment?'

The captain started to respond, but Winston held up a hand and shook his head. 'We are finished here, Officer Jones. Close the door on the way out.'

After Leighton had gone, Captain Pierce sat down opposite the chief.

'I said it after he left his post and vanished to check on his kid, he's emotionally unstable. Now he's deliberately fucking up investigations – he's a liability, sir,' Pierce said, 'we should get rid of him before he does any more damage.'

The chief sighed and then looked at the captain.

'If it comes to that,' he said, firmly, 'it'll be my decision, Steven, not yours. This isn't open season on Leighton! Do you understand?'

'Yes, sir.' Pierce said, quietly.

44

As he left the airless corridor of the management area of the station, Leighton encountered Lisa heading out of the small dispatch room. Leighton felt some of his frustration thaw when he saw a friendly face.

'Hey, officer,' she said with a tired but genuine smile, 'you about to start the day?'

'Yeah,' Leighton said. 'How about you?'

'Just finished. Been on since ten last night.' Lisa yawned.

'Eventful night?'

'Nope, just a couple of calls came in on an attempted break in down at the harbour and a minor collision on the Freeway.'

'That's busy enough,' Leighton said with a smile. 'Listen, I'm just heading down to admin, you want to stop off at the canteen for a coffee to help wake you up?'

'Sure,' Lisa nodded, 'but can we take them outside, I'm getting withdrawal symptoms from lack of sunlight.'

As they sat at one of the two park benches located on a patch of grass outside the station, Leighton and Lisa sipped their drinks and watched the passing traffic drifting along Mission Avenue.

'So, how's it going,' he said as he sat down, 'you starting to feel like you've been here for years?'

'Still the new girl at present. In my experience of working dispatch that lasts for a year or so,' Lisa said with a shrug, 'but it's better than my last station – that's for sure. So, you not heading out on the road today?'

'Nope, I have to kick around here, apparently. I'm in the doghouse,' Leighton said. 'They've got me doing paperwork for the next couple of days as a punishment.'

'Punishment for what?' Lisa asked.

'Looking into some other team's case.'

'What case?'

'Tina Blanchette.'

There was a moment of silence, which suggested to Leighton that Lisa was already aware of his unwelcome involvement.

'I thought that investigation was all wrapped up, I heard from Marie that it had been confirmed that the girl was up in Alaska with her dad – case closed'

'Yeah.' Leighton winked. 'I guess that's what they're telling everyone.'

'You genuinely don't think so?' Lisa asked. Her tone of voice suggested that she was satisfied with the official account.

'Nope.' Leighton took a sip of his coffee.

'What do you think happened?'

'You really want to know?' he glanced at her.

'I wouldn't ask otherwise, I really want to know.'

Leighton sighed. 'Well, I think the kid was possibly abducted by somebody, and that she somehow got away from them. But to tell you the truth, Lisa, I get the feeling that you know this already. Police stations are small little communities and word spreads like wildfire around here. So, I'm thinking that somebody has already filled you in about my position. Am I right?'

The younger woman suddenly blushed and looked at her feet. 'Yes, a little.'

'So, are you trying to catch me out, win some points with the chief?'

'No, it's not like that.'

'So why you asking these questions?'

Lisa looked back up at Leighton. 'Teddy Leach has been making a habit of coming into the dispatch area at the end of his shifts. He likes to complain that he is doing all the work whilst you get paid for a being an unstable liability.'

'Nice.' Leighton chuckled.

'He also told me to stay the hell away from you.'

'So what are you doing sitting here sipping coffee with an unstable liability?' Leighton asked.

'I reckon I'm not very good at being told what to do,' Lisa said with a self-conscious smile.

'Well I guess that makes two of us.'

'Look, I wasn't trying to catch you out. I just wanted to know your theory. Why you are so opposed to the official line of enquiry?'

'Well, my theory seems to be just as possible as any other theory.'

'Okay, so if this kid escaped her abductor why hasn't she shown up somewhere, flagged down a car or something like that?'

'I don't know,' Leighton shrugged and took another drink, 'maybe she's hurt. She might even show up dead, but not in Alaska.'

Lisa frowned for a moment and appeared to be lost in some private recollection.

'You know about eight years ago, in my first year in San Bernardino, we had something similar to this. It was pretty horrible.'

'What do you mean?' Leighton sounded suddenly more alert.

'A couple of young girls died that year. I remember how much it freaked me out because Stan and I were thinking about starting a family, and I kept thinking that the world wasn't a safe place to do that. Anyway, after these two girls were found, everyone said their deaths were accidental, except one old cop. When I heard Teddy Leach going on about you, I figured you were maybe a little bit like that guy.'

'Can you remember his name?'

'Oh yeah.' Lisa nodded. 'Len Wells. He retired that same year, partly because nobody was listening to him, but mainly because the people at the top wanted rid of him. Seems like nobody wants a rogue cop running around sharing a crazy theory.'

'What was his crazy theory?' Leighton asked.

Lisa hesitated for a moment, clearly unsure if sharing the information would help Leighton or not.

'Come on.' He smiled. 'I'm already waist deep in this.'

'You could be worse,' Lisa said.

'What up to my neck?'

'This guy lost his job.'

'Why?'

'He thought that a serial killer abducted then murdered the girls.'

After a moment, Leighton looked directly at the younger woman.

'Do you know where I could find this guy?' he asked.

45

As he leaned on the reception desk of Sunbeam Garden Retirement Village, Leighton glanced around at the various pamphlets neatly arranged in fan shapes on the veneered surface. Many of them were advertising low impact exercise classes for more mature persons; others were promoting local golf facilities offering discounts to elderly golfers. A cheap plastic fan was droning nearby, causing the edges of the pamphlets to flutter like leaves in an autumn breeze. A tall, young man with neat bleached hair and sculpted eyebrows had been flicking through a copy of *Vanity Fair* when Leighton arrived, but he quickly folded it neatly over and smiled at him.

'How may I help you?' he asked, cheerfully.

'I'm looking to visit one of your residents,' Leighton said.

'Which one of our guests is it that you're interested in seeing?'

'Len Wells,' Leighton said, hoping it was the right place.

'Give me one moment please.'

The young man turned away from Leighton and peered at a large A3 spreadsheet pinned on the wall behind the reception area. He then moved a manicured nail down each name in turn.

'There we go,' he said without turning around. 'Mr Wells is in number seventy-seven. That's in the Rose complex. Have you visited our retirement village before?'

'No – first time,' Leighton replied.

'Here.' The young man turned back to the desk and rummaged around for a moment. He then handed Leighton a small map printed on peach coloured paper. 'The numbers and areas are clearly shown. Each area is named after a flower and the colours of the buildings match it – so the Cornflower buildings are purple and the Buttercup ones are yellow.'

'I get it,' Leighton said with a smile. 'It's a nice touch.'

'Well, the colours are a little faded, but if you have any problems just pop back here and I'll walk you round.'

'Thanks,' Leighton said with a small nod of his head, 'much appreciated.'

Leighton left the air-conditioned reception and let the screen door wheeze closed behind him. It was a warm afternoon and the walk through the retirement village was a pleasant one. The entire place comprised a square mile of neat pastel-collared homes organised in small squares of homes with dipping pools at the centre of each. Leighton noted with a small smile that the pavement snaking through the place was a faded yellow colour. He guessed that the residents of this place would be old enough to remember *The Wizard of Oz* movie and perhaps appreciate the notion that there might be some place nice waiting over the rainbow.

As he peered around at each collection of small houses, Leighton checked the numbers on the door of each property against the map.

Eventually, as the sun was starting to scorch the back of his neck, Leighton found number seventy-seven located at the northern end of the park. This section backed on the Amtrak Train Line which ran all the way north to Los Angeles. Leighton figured that the rent at this end of the park was most probably twenty percent cheaper, unless the residents attracted to the regular clattering rhythm of the trains. Wells' home was a neat, rose-coloured building with a narrow western style porch. There were only two items upon it – a rocking chair and a discarded aluminium walking frame.

Leighton stepped up to the flaking red door and pressed the buzzer.

There was a shuffling noise and some muffled cursing from inside. Eventually, the door opened a couple of inches and a watchful eye appeared.

'Who the hell are you?' a gravelly voice asked.

'Sir, my name is Leighton Jones. I'm sorry to disturb you. I was wondering if I could speak to you for a few minutes.'

'You selling something?' The door seemed to close a fraction.

'No, sir, I'm not.'

'Didn't think so. Salesmen and bible thumpers always look good; you look like shit. You a cop?'

'Yeah,' Leighton said, 'well recognised.'

'Where's your badge?' the man behind the door asked.

Leighton reached into his back pocket and took out the black leather wallet containing his gold metal badge and ID. He held it up to the gap so the man could inspect it.

The elderly man screwed up his eye as he peered. Eventually, he let out a sigh suggesting the exercise was pretty useless.

'Looks legit but my eyes can't read any letters smaller than a newspaper headline. So how come you never showed it at the start?'

'I'm not here officially,' Leighton said.

'Not official?' The old man blew out a wheezy breath. 'So, what the hell do you want?'

'I'm a friend of Lisa Martinez,' Leighton said, 'I was hoping you could give me a couple of minutes to speak about Marianne Hume.'

There was a flicker of something in the eye watching Leighton.

'Why you chasing that shit? It's old news.'

'Yeah, I know, but Lisa told me you had a theory about the suspect.'

'The kid is dead and my bullshit theories aren't going to change that.'

'They might,' Leighton offered.

'What difference is it to you?' the man on the other side of the door asked. 'You one of those sickos who get off on hearing this stuff or something?'

'No, it's nothing weird.' Leighton held up his hand. 'I'm looking into a case. I just want to know what you found out.'

'Have a good day, son.'

The door had already clicked firmly shut before Leighton got a chance to respond, but he refused to quit. He made a fist and banged it on the door, then he put his face so close to the surface it looked as if he was about to kiss it.

'I think the guy you were investigating has taken another kid,' Leighton called. 'I think she's still alive but she won't be for much longer unless I can figure it out, so I need your help Mr Wells. Can you hear me? He's taken another one – she's seven years old.'

There was a long moment of silence during which Leighton suspected he had made a mistake coming to the place. Then he heard a rattle, and the door slowly opened to reveal a large man dressed in a golf shirt and chinos. His face was prickly with stubble and his hair stood up in tufts that suggested to Leighton that his arrival had interrupted this guy's siesta.

'Well, in that case I reckon you better come in.'

46

The stranger had walked aimlessly, pushing his flatbed trolley down the aisle of Northwood Hunting Supplies twice without any success. The place was a cavernous warehouse filled with everything a person would need to hunt and kill pretty much anything. Whilst this was appealing to him on a personal level, he also didn't like the idea of others being able to come to places like this and gain the same power as him. It made him seem less special, and he didn't like that at all.

The stranger's lack of success in the store wasn't because it was poorly laid out – which it was. Rather, he had been lost in thought. He was remembering how he had almost been caught moments after he murdered his first victim.

He had been parked at the top floor of a multi-storey car park in Winchester sixteen years earlier. It had been a Thursday afternoon in September. At the time, the place was not as busy, and he could have parked anywhere he wanted, but he always liked the view from tall buildings. The stranger had been smoking a cigarette and admiring the view from seven floors up, when the kid had just appeared out of nowhere and stood at his side – he looked about seven or eight; all stick legs and energy. The stranger glanced around to see where the boy had come from, but there were no other cars parked on that level. He must have taken the elevator up just for the view. The boy had been standing on the tiptoes of his baseball boots trying to get a better look when, without saying a word, the stranger grabbed him and propelled him straight over the edge. Without even looking to see the consequences of his actions, the stranger simply crushed his cigarette, got straight into his car and drove down the maddening spiral ramp and out of the place.

He carefully monitored the news in the days that followed, but there was nothing about the incident on the TV. Eventually, he read a small piece in the *Valley Chronicle* about the fatal accident. It apparently sparked a campaign to have safety rails fitted to the top of all multi-storey parking facilities in the area. Despite the reassuring verdict, for months afterwards the stranger had been sure he would eventually be caught. That was why he moved to Lancaster then San Bernardino, but of course each move only resulted in more victims. This time, he had concluded that if he took just one victim and didn't get rid of them straight away, he would perhaps not feel the urge to get more. But now she had gone and spoiled everything.

The sound of an announcement over the speaker system shook him from his thoughts, and he found the aisle filled with the items he was looking for. There were hundreds of traps available, but the ones the stranger was particularly looking for were square jaw spring traps. The largest ones were on the bottom shelves of the aisle, stacked vertically because of their size and weight. Using both hands, the stranger grunted as he lifted the first of four steel traps on to the trolley.

47

Len Wells led Leighton into a small cramped living room and pointed to a round dining table with two wooden chairs pushed into the corner of the room.

'You can park your ass there. No point getting too comfy.'

'Thank you.' Leighton sat down.

While his host vanished out of the room, Leighton thought perhaps he had gone to get some type of refreshment, but instead Len shuffled back into the room carrying a black box file.

'They wanted me to hand back everything I had,' he said as he slowly sat down opposite Leighton. 'Fuck that! Nobody was interested anyway. This is everything that I found on what was happening at the time, and if I hadn't grabbed it, the whole file would have sat on a basement shelf till judgement day. I reckon the bosses just didn't want me figuring out stuff that they couldn't.'

'Were you working missing persons at the time?'

'No, and I guess that was the problem,' Len said with a wry smile.

'What do you mean?'

'I was sniffing around somebody else's case. That meant nobody in the station would listen to what I had to say. Eventually, they said I was obstructive and I got retired out at fifty-eight years old.'

'How long ago was that?'

'Eight years ago, give or take. I kind of lost track of time after I lost my wife. But anyhow, everything I've got is here. So, what do you want to know?'

'Anything you've got.'

'I was worried you were going to say that.' Len sighed and stood up. He shuffled out of the room, and returned with a half empty bottle of Jim Beam Bourbon and a mug with a faded Planet Hollywood logo printed on it. As he sat down, he unscrewed the cap and poured a shot into the mug. 'I ain't a drunk, son. This stuff is just the sweetest way to kill the pain in my joints. You want some?'

'No, I'm good thanks,' Leighton said.

'Good, this stuff's not cheap,' Leon said and took a sip from his mug. 'Right, this is how it went down. In eighty-seven I was working vice in San Bernardino. That summer a nine-year-old called Betty Tulin went missing. At the time, nobody in the station seemed too uptight about it. It was just another report to fill in then a matter of waiting.'

'How come?'

'Some detective in missing persons established that the kid had already run away a couple of times before. She lived in a cheap apartment block alongside six siblings and a violent father – I'd probably have run away too. Anyhow, given the kid's history, they figured she would most likely show up after a couple of days, like she had done before.'

'But she didn't?' Leighton asked.

'No, she did… kind of.' Wells opened the box file and rummaged his had around in it like a magician mixing up cards, before finally producing a small photograph and handing it to Leighton. 'Some worker at the Redlands Wastewater Treatment facility fished her body out of the Santa Anna River. They figured she must have been playing somewhere near the edge of the water and fallen in. Absolute bullshit, of course.'

Leighton glanced down at the photograph of the thin, pale figure lying face down on the river bank like a strange dead fish. He was happy to move his eyes anywhere else.

'When you're a cop, you think the badge makes you immune to the stuff you see. But some crimes – the bad ones – they stick to you,' Wells said, quietly. 'I reckon they stain you – like a messed-up tattoo.'

Leighton dragged his eyes away from the image. 'You don't think it was possible that she could have fallen in?'

'Yeah.' Wells chuckled bitterly. 'It's *possible*, but so is winning the State Lottery. Doesn't mean I'm booking myself on the next first-class flight to Vegas.'

'So, what's your theory?' Leighton asked.

For a moment Wells said nothing. He simply looked at the stained tiled floor of his tiny retirement home. Leighton suspected that the older man had not shared his story for a long time. Eventually Wells sighed, then spoke up.

'She was picked up. Simple as that. The Tulin home was six miles north from the river. No kid is going to walk six miles to play in some river – certainly not on their own.'

'Any witnesses?'

'No. Betty said that after supper her sister had gone out to catch fireflies in a jam jar. She said that she would often do this along the road that ran by their home.'

'What else was on the road?' Leighton asked.

'Nothing – two miles of nothing but bushes and telegraph poles.'

'What did the autopsy say?'

'Cause of death was drowning. She had most likely been in the water since the day she went missing. Whether or not she was dead when she had gone into the water could apparently not be confirmed.'

'So not a homicide?'

'Not officially,' Len Wells said, tapping the side of his nose.

'You said you were working in vice at the time. How did you get involved in the case?'

'About a month after the kid was found I arrested a guy in a drugs raid on a local pool bar. His name was Joelle Hilson and we got him with a bag of cocaine in every pocket. Anyway, as I was driving him back to the station house this guy told me that he could give me some information about Betty Tulin if I could get his charges dropped. I told him I was listening but I couldn't promise anything.'

'What did he tell you?'

'This was a guy who spent most of his week dealing in bars. He said he'd played pool in a biker bar with some young guy who got drunker as the night went on. He said there was a TV above the bar and when a news report came on, the young guy started mumbling that he had killed the kid, and the cops would never catch him.'

'Did you put his claims into your arrest report?'

'Sure,' Wells sighed, 'but my captain told me to redact it.'

'Why?' Leighton asked.

'He said I had an unreliable witness trying to squirm out of a fistful of drugs charges. I wasn't even that convinced of the guy's claims at the time. But there was something that stuck with me.'

'What was it?'

'The dealer told me that before he had left the bar that night, the young guy said he was going to do it again.'

'Marianne Hume?'

'Damn right! Do you know much about her?'

Leighton shook his head. 'Just that it seemed to take months for her body to finally turn up.'

'Nine months. She was taken from her school in October, and her body wasn't found until the following July.' Wells absently rubbed his temple as he spoke. 'I knew it was the same guy. I felt it in my bones. It was like he was getting better at hiding his victims.'

'What do you mean?'

'Betty seemed like she was disposed of in a panic. But Marianne was found in a remote location, like he was being careful.'

'So, what did you do?'

'What any cop does – I gathered evidence. On my day off, I took a drive to see Hilson, who was halfway through an eight-month stretch in West Valley county jail. I wanted to get his claims on the record, and see if he could remember anything else. But I guess all that shit he shovelled up his nose didn't help any because he couldn't give me a description of the guy in the bar – other than he was skinny. But he did tell me something vital.'

'What was it?'

'He said that the young guy had been driving a brown or rust coloured car – a sedan. So, I went digging around.'

'Officially?'

'Nope, it wasn't my case. Hell, it wasn't even my jurisdiction. But when a cop shows up with a badge and some questions, nobody's interested in which specific department you're from. Anyway, I talked with the families and to some neighbours, and what do you know… witnesses in both the Betty Tulin and the Marianne Hume case reported seeing a reddish-brown sedan in the area prior to the abduction. Marianne's younger sister even told her family that a couple of days she had been followed home from school by a guy in a chocolate coloured car.'

'Jeez, didn't that convince your colleagues?'

'No, son. In our line of work you are expected to follow the rules – even if the rules are wrong. By going digging into somebody else's case you put yourself outside of the club, and once you're out you don't get back in – ever. I took what I had to my superiors – let them know that I thought the kids had been taken.'

'I take it they wouldn't listen?'

'They told me to fuck off. Said I was impeding an on-going investigation.'

'So, what was their theory of what happened?'

'The department was big on gang activity that year, so a couple of missing girls from the wrong side of the tracks didn't warrant the spending of too many tax dollars. Betty's death was put down to accidental drowning and Marianne was officially recorded as unexplained, but Betty… she was believed to have wandered off.'

Leighton frowned. 'I don't know much about her case, what happened to her?'

'Vanished while out for a picnic with her parents. They had gone fishing at Chino Creek – it's mostly wooded down there and pretty swampy too; looks more like Louisiana than California.

Marianne who was eight at the time had her own fishing rod and was fairly capable according to her folks.'

'Did she wander off?'

'She needed to pee. Her mom told me that Marianne propped up her rod against a tree, and stepped back into the bushes. She and Marianne's dad kept their attention on their own lines for five or ten minutes but when their daughter didn't come back, they started shouting on her. You got any kids?'

'Yeah.' Leighton nodded, slowly. 'I have a daughter – she's seven.'

'Then you know how her folks would've felt when they had been standing there in the creek shouting for a while without getting any answer. They told me that they abandoned their rods to get pulled away into the water while they began searching. Didn't do any good of course; she was long gone by then.'

'Where was she found?'

'Up in Angelus Oaks – sixty miles from where she was last seen. Nothing up there but tall trees and telegraph poles. A long way away for a kid to walk. Sound familiar?'

'Yeah,' Leighton said in a dry whisper. 'You said that cars were seen in the area when the girls went missing. Did anybody get a licence number?'

'Nope, nobody knew it meant anything.'

'If it was him, the suspect took a risk using the same car.'

'Yeah, but my theory is that he only ever lifted a couple of kids from any given area. I think he took two kids in that patch then moved on. By the time anybody sees a pattern he's already gone.'

'You think there were others, before the Tulin and Hume girls?'

'Yeah, of course there were others,' Wells said. His tone suggested it would be crazy to suggest otherwise.

'How many?' Leighton asked.

Wells took a while to answer. He poured another shot of bourbon into his mug, took a slow sip of it and then looked at the floor. 'Four that I'm certain of.' He dragged a veined hand across his stubble-peppered face. 'I know there could even be more, but those four were officially his.'

'Why are you so sure there are more?'

'Nobody wakes up one day and decides to start taking and killing kids in a way that means they get away with it every time. They would get caught. But not this guy. He knows what he's doing. Victims are all kids yeah, but other than that there's no real pattern. We have different ages, race, gender, social class, location and M.O.'

'So, what makes you so sure they were all connected at all?'

'Jeez – you sound like my old chief. He couldn't see it – the dumb fuck. He had the power to stop the killer but he was too dumb to realise it. I kept at him, gave him all the stuff I had, but it's like he was colour-blind and I was asking him to look at a rainbow. How long have you been a cop?'

'Fourteen years.'

'Well, I reckon after most guys have put in twelve on the streets, they're pretty switched on in terms of how to do the job. In my final days at San Bernardino I had put in thirty-eight years.'

'That's a long shift,' Leighton said with a smile.

'The chief had done thirteen, and my captain only had six – but of course he had two degrees from UCLA. Anyway, those two bozos had half my experience between them.'

'I guess that's why they couldn't see it.'

'That's the truth, son.'

'Listen, there's a seven-year-girl who's missing from her home near Oceanside. Her friend said she was talking to a man who had a brown coloured car.'

'Shit.' Wells looked at the floor, his shoulders slumping. 'I had somehow convinced myself that he had stopped – had died or maybe got locked up for something else.'

'What should I do?' Leighton asked.

'Jeez, son, how the hell do I know? I'm a washed-up ex-cop with a bad hip and a drink problem.'

'But you were on to him before, Len. Nobody else seems to even know that this guy exists, but you were onto him. I'm out of my depth here.'

'I guess you are,' Wells said with a deep sigh.

'Look, I just need to know how to get closer to this psycho. I can try to dig up some evidence.'

'Okay, I'll tell you something. God knows if it'll help you find the kid, but it's all I've got. Look for a guy with his own car, who lives out of the way. If any people were around him, they would have noticed his weirdness by now. I know society has changed since I was a kid. People don't look out for each other the way they used to, but they still notice cars coming and going or people acting kind of weird. Where did your missing kid go missing from?'

'Fallbrook. She had been playing in a creek outside the family home.'

'If that's where he snatched her, then your guy is likely to be living on the edge of the city or nearby. On a ranch maybe. Somewhere fairly isolated. That way he can avoid neighbours noticing things.'

Leighton nodded as he scratched at his notepad.

I reckon there's something else you should consider, something important,' Wells said, quietly.

'What's that?'

'This guy will have seen the kid at home before, have watched them in some way. I guarantee it.'

'You sure?'

'I am.' Wells nodded, and took a sip of his drink.

'How do you know?'

'He doesn't fuck up. If anybody's doing anything for the first time – even basic stuff like baking a cake or stripping a car engine – they're going make a couple of mistakes at least. This guy doesn't. That tells me that he has had practised. If he snatched the kid from near her home, like he did with the others, then he planned it.'

'Did you discover any other cases that might've been his?'

'I thought that I did, but once they got me out of service I was just like every other civilian. I only heard the same news stories as everybody else. There were a couple that got my attention. But you're still a lawman. That means you can go digging without anyone getting suspicious.'

'Well except for my colleagues in missing persons.'

'Hell, let them worry about that. You're doing their job for them, the bastards should thank you for it. You just need to get busy hunting this prick down, before he takes another one and moves on again.'

'Where would you start?'

Len Wells picked up his glass and took a slow sip. He then glanced at Leighton. 'Are you serious about this; not just as a little side interest – but serious enough to get bloody?'

'I guess I am,' Leighton said, quietly.

'I'd start with the last known location. This guy doesn't just lift kids at random, he knows where they live, and grabs them close to it. That's what makes me think he either lives nearby or is able to stake out their home for a while before the actual attack. If you confirm the location then look for anybody with priors or warrants who lives in the area. Somebody who has moved there in the last year or so.'

'You've really helped me,' Leighton said with a smile. He got up and moved to the door. 'I don't know what to say.'

Wells grunted as he stood up too, then shuffled after Leighton. 'Don't say anything, just save the kid.'

'I'll try, I promise,' Leighton said. He then opened the door and squinted against the light.

'You sure you don't want a shot of bourbon before you go?' Wells asked.

'No thanks, I don't drink spirits.'

'You will,' Wells said as he closed the door.

48

As he walked up the cracked path leading to the door of the property on the opposite side of the street from the Blanchette home, Leighton stared down the building. A disembowelled car sat in the drive, propped up on cinder blocks like some dead beast. Following his meeting with Len Wells, Leighton had stopped off at the station and ran a prior conviction and warrants check on the small cluster of houses. He had struck gold with one of them.

Leighton pressed the doorbell, heard an angry buzz from somewhere further back in the house.

Eventually, a short scruffy-looking man appeared on the other side of the screen door. He made no attempt to open it.

'You Ronald Draper?' Leighton asked.

'What d'you want?'

'I'd like to speak to you.' Leighton said.

'Fuck off!'

'Officially,' Leighton said and held up his badge.

The guy showed no change in expression, but he immediately folded his arms. This informed Leighton that this was someone accustomed to confrontation with cops.

'What d'you want to know?' he asked.

'About a missing person.'

'That kid from across the street?'

'That's right.' Leighton nodded. 'You know about that?'

'Sure, your cop buddy came knocking on doors yesterday. Jeez, don't you ever speak to each other. Well, I've got nothing to say. That shit's got nothing to do with me.'

'I didn't say it had,' Leighton said and waited, patiently, deliberately.

'You were charged with rape in Lewisham.'

'Hey, those charges were dropped. She was my girlfriend and she got pissed at me for doing it with her cousin. It's all in the police report. Check it out if you want.'

'Where were you on Monday afternoon?' Leighton asked.

'Work.'

'Can anybody else verify that?'

'Sure, my asshole boss and forty other guys who work in the Street Maintenance crew. I worked an eight our shift. My boss is Chuck Wheeler. Feel free to speak to him.'

'I will,' Leighton said and walked away.

***

When Leighton approached his car he glanced around. He was trying to get a sense of what had happened on the day Tina vanished. The problem was that with the exception of Ronald Draper's place and an elderly neighbour's bungalow, there only were three other houses – Tina's and those of her two other neighbours. All of the residents checked out, and there were no other buildings nearby. Leighton couldn't see how Len Wells' notion of somebody else being involved could apply. There wasn't even a bus stop or grocery store that might give people reason to hang around. The case felt more hopeless than ever, and he knew he would end up letting Angela Blanchette and her daughter down too. He opened the car door and was about to get in when he paused.

It was at that moment in the heat of the afternoon that Leighton's eye caught a momentary glint of metal at the top of a telegraph pole on the opposite side of the road.

Leaving the car door half open, Leighton hurried across the hot road and stood beneath the wooden pole. Holding up his hand to shield his eyes, he peered directly at the box. It was square and made of polished metal. Leighton estimated that it had only been there for a couple of weeks at most. Stepping back, he peered at the surrounding houses, then back at the pole.

Judging by the position of it, anybody who was up a ladder leaning against the pole or sitting in a cherry picker would be able to see for miles around. But more disturbingly they would be looking down directly into the gardens of the three houses, they would be looking directly down on Tina and her friends and they would be able to see into the windows of these houses too.

After crouching down, Leighton took a notepad from his pocket and then carefully copied the identity number of the post, then hurried back to his car.

49

Captain Steven Pierce, who having just secured a promotion to a different city, was no longer as emotionally invested in Oceanside. He had already begun the painful task of organising his paperwork in preparation for the inevitable handover to his replacement. Having spent most of the day up to his eyes in bench warrants and lapsed parking fines, he had just grabbed a coffee and was returning to his office when he was confronted by Captain Levvy in the administration corridor.

'Hey, Ellen,' he said. 'How's your day?'

'Good,' she replied, 'I heard you got the San Diego job. Congratulations. What did that interview involve – four parts?'

'Thanks. It was five actually.'

'Ouch,' she said with a wincing smile. 'So, when you starting?'

'A couple of weeks, unless the chief can pull some strings and speed things up.'

'I'm sure it'll just fly by. Hey listen, before you go, can you do something for me?'

'Sure what?' Pierce took a sip, to conceal his dismay at something else to add to his list.

'Can you keep Leighton Jones on a tighter leash?'

'What do you mean?'

'He's still messing with our investigation of the Blanchette kid's disappearance. He's been all over it like a rash. The guy obviously doesn't know when to back the fuck off.'

'Shit! Sorry, Ellen. He thinks he's Colombo. I'll get on his back.'

'Thanks, Steve, I appreciate it.'

50

Leighton pulled into the parking lot of the Oceanside Gas and Electric Company. It was a cube-shaped brick building surrounded by a variety of pickup trucks and cherry pickers. All of them were white and featured the yellow OGEC badge on every side. A high security fence running around the edge of the parking lot gave the place a sense of being zoo-like, as if the vehicles might plan a rebellion and try to escape.

After locking up his car, Leighton entered the building and approached reception area where a tall man in a blue boiler suit was pouring over an oil stained truck parts catalogue.

'If you want to report a fault, you need to go through the switchboard,' he said without looking up.

'I'm from Oceanside P.D.,' Leighton said whilst holding his badge.

The tall man looked up in alarm and flipped the catalogue closed. 'Sorry, we get so used to members of the public coming in here to report a blown hairdryer socket. I'm Ned Murphy – shift manager here. What can I do for you today?'

Leighton pushed his open notepad across the counter. 'I want to speak to whoever carried out the replacement of this transformer within the last few weeks.'

The man reached out one finger and quietly read the numbers to himself. Eventually he looked back up at Leighton.

'Sure, I know who was out there doing the repair. It was Eddie Craven, but I'm afraid you can't speak to him.'

'I can get a warrant,' Leighton said, hoping that his bluff was convincing. It was seriously unlikely that he could get any judge to approve a warrant based on the little evidence he had.

'Makes no difference if you have a warrant or not,' Ned Murphy said, indifferently, 'Eddie hasn't been in all this week – called in sick on Monday morning. To be honest, if he stays off into next week he won't be working here at all.'

'How long has he been employed here?' Leighton asked.

'Little less than a year,' the man replied with a shrug.

'You know where he was based before that?'

'Hard to be sure.' Murphy scratched his head. 'According to what he's told us, the guy's been all over. Likes moving around, I guess. Mentioned a bunch of different places.'

'Was San Bernardino among those places?'

'Yeah.' Ned nodded. 'He said he stayed there. A while back.'

Leighton felt a sense of growing unease.

'You got a current address for him?' Leighton asked. His voice sounded steady but he felt like he had just stepped into a snake pit.

The guy nodded and took out a distressed black A4 notebook from under the counter. He laid it flat then copied out the address on to an orange Post-it note and handed it to Leighton.

'Can you do one other thing for me, Ned?' Leighton said as he headed to the door.

'Sure.'

'If Craven gets back in touch, don't mention I was here.'

'Sure, I won't say a word.'

'You're a good man,' Leighton said and left.

When he got outside, Leighton glanced around until he found what he was looking for. After hurrying out of the depot parking lot, he approached a battered phone booth and pulled out his notepad. Flipping through the pages he found the number he needed. He picked up the handset and punched the number into the keypad.

It rang for only a moment before it was picked up.

'Hello?' Angela Blanchette sounded like a woman who was gradually sinking out of existence.

'Mrs Blanchette, its Leighton Jones. I haven't found Tina, but I need to ask you something.'

'What?' her voice sounded hopeless as if she was calling from a raft drifting out to sea. Leighton wondered if someone had possibly medicated her for her own good.

'Do you remember somebody working on the electrical wires outside your house in recent weeks?'

There was a long pause. Then eventually a memory surfaced in the woman's foggy mind.

'Yeah, actually there was a van with one of those little crane things on the back. I think the guy was repairing something.'

'When was this?'

'About two weeks ago, maybe.'

'Did Tina speak to the guy?'

'Oh, Jesus – is that him? Is that who's got my baby?'

'Angela, did Tina speak to him?'

'I don't know,' she said between sobs, 'I don't know.'

'Angela, I want you to listen to me, I know where he lives and I'm going there right now so you've just got to trust me. Can you do that?'

'Yes,' she sobbed.

'Good, I'll be in touch.'

51

Len Wells sat at his small table with a glass in his hand and the black box file closed in front of him. He had used duct tape to seal the whole thing up. With its black shape, scuffed surface and sealed edges, the box reminded him of an object from a Shirley Jackson story he had read in *The New Yorker* just after the war; about a town where everyone stones to death one of the residents every year as part of an ancient ritual. Nobody even remembered why they did – it was just a tradition.

At the time, Len couldn't believe that right-minded people would tolerate such a thing in a civil society. But after thirty-six years on the job, he realised that people would just about tolerate anything if it didn't affect them personally.

Len winced as a sudden flash of pain ripped through his body. He closed his eyes for a moment until it passed. When the pain had subsided, he picked up his glass and took a long drink of bourbon.

With trembling hands, he folded a sheet of paper in half and then taped it to the top of the box. His final step involved using a thick Sharpie pen to write on the neat white rectangle of paper:

Care of Leighton Jones.

52

Leighton was no longer interested in propriety and would have kicked the door open if it had been required. But he didn't want to alert Craven. Having pulled on a pair of latex gloves, he tried the door of Craven's trailer. When he found that it was locked, he crouched down on the rubber doormat and began using a small pick set to unlock it. In a decade of getting into locked cars abandoned along the highways, he had become highly skilled at using the tiny hooks and pins.

The lock clicked open.

Once inside, Leighton discovered that the place was baking hot but other than that it looked fairly tidy. Leighton pulled out his gun and removed the safety. Having a locked door and no car suggested the place was empty but he wasn't taking any chances. He moved cautiously through the trailer from front to back. The neat living room led to a central section with a kitchen on one side and shower room on the other. There was a bedroom at the back with not much else. If Tina had been here, there wasn't any sign of her now. But that meant that Craven had tidied the place, so Leighton knew that any clues would most likely be in one specific area.

Stepping outside, Leighton let the door click locked behind him. He then walked down the two trailer steps and saw what he was looking for.

A few feet away from the building, in a chicken wire enclosure, sat a metal trashcan with a dented lid. Leighton holstered his gun, then walked over to it. After pulling off the lid, he let it clatter, like a giant dime to the dusty ground. Leighton found himself looking at a black plastic sack, tied at the neck. He took his time untying the bag, then – once it was open – he rummaged inside hoping to find some item of clothing or perhaps some candy; anything that might relate to Tina. Instead, all he found were crushed beer cans. But beneath them was a crushed piece of paper. After fishing it out Leighton unfolded the paper and squinted –*Pembleton Farm*.

Leighton frowned as he stared at the words. The name reminded him of Camp Pendleton – a nearby marine base, but this was spelled differently and Leighton knew from personal experience that there was no farm on the base.

He returned the items to the bag, tied it and placed the lid back in place.

As he climbed into his car, Leighton decided that the best place to find out this farm's location was back at the station. However as he drove away, Leighton was unaware that his presence had being noted by Ralph Byars-the owner of the park- who lowered his binoculars and stepped back into his own trailer. By the time Leighton had left the trailer park, Byars was already on the telephone to the police.

53

He stared at the road atlas for the area under the index – but found nothing. Luckily for Leighton, the traffic department of Oceanside P.D. had maps going back sixty years or further to when the city was little more than a fishing harbour. He visited the archive area, located the shelf and pulled three of them covering the area around Old Mill Way from archives and now sat at his cluttered desk. Two of the maps had no mention of Pembleton Farm, but the last one did. It showed two small buildings surrounded by a crescent-shaped hill. Leighton heard his heart beat thumping in his ear.

After getting up from his desk, he crossed the office area to the large photocopier and ran off a couple of prints of the section. Returning to the desk he took out a red Sharpie and drew a circle around the farm on both copies.

Leighton then stepped into Levvy's office and held the map out as if it was a peace offering.

She was sitting at the desk typing, looked up at him but said nothing.

'Captain, I know I've been a pain in the ass, but if only to humour me, can you please direct some resources to this area. This is where she's likely to be.'

'What are you talking about?' Levvy stared at his outstretched hand.

'I know where she is,' he said.

'Based on what?' the captain asked with a frown, 'some hunch?' Levvy took the map and glanced down at it and then back at Leighton.

'I saw her in that area marked on the map,' Leighton said, firmly. 'Really, that's enough.'

'You don't know that you saw her; you saw somebody in that area. So, you're instinct is not enough to justify using valuable resources.'

'Look, that's not all – I found the home address of a guy who might be the suspect. His name is Edward Craven, he works for OGEC doing line repairs. He did a job in Fallbrook a couple of weeks ago. It all fits!'

'You were told to let this whole thing go,' Levvy said, firmly.

'I know that, captain. But I'm only asking for this one thing. Then I'll let it go.'

'Look, give me a minute to speak to the chief, I'll see what he's willing to approve.' Levvy stood up. 'You sit right there.'

'Thanks, captain, I appreciate this.' Leighton sighed.

When she was gone, Leighton gazed out of the small window and smiled. It had taken a while and he hoped to God it wasn't too late, but at least now somebody was listening to him. If they could put a helicopter out with a paramedic, there was still a chance that they could save the little girl.

Eventually, the office door opened, but it was Chief Winston rather than Levvy who looked in.

'Hi, Leighton, can you come through next door for a moment?'

Chief Winston entered the room ahead of Leighton and sat behind the dark wooden desk. There was no seat for Leighton who remained standing.

'Did Levvy explain the situation, sir?'

'She did indeed,' Winston said.

Leighton crossed the room and began to sit, but the chief held up a hand to stop him. The table between them was empty with the exception of a glass paperweight, a graduation photograph of the chief's daughter and a blank sheet of A4 paper.

'Don't bother sitting, this will only take a minute.'

'Okay,' Leighton said, unable to gauge the chief's tone.

'Captain Levvy had already come to speak to me at our team debrief yesterday and informed me that she feels you are disobeying instruction and continually harassing her over the Blanchette case. Obviously, your actions in confronting her again today confirms this.'

'Sir, I was only trying to—' Leighton was silenced by the chief holding up a hand.

'Against my better judgement – and in an effort to get your mind back on your job – yesterday afternoon I approved a night-time sweep of the area you specified, for six miles running south from the location of your sighting using a helicopter.'

Leighton felt his heart rate suddenly increase. 'What did they find?'

'Nothing, they found absolutely nada. Do you know what that means?'

'No.' Leighton couldn't think straight. If there was no heat signature, then Tina may already be dead.

'I thought as much.' Winston shook his head gravely. 'It means – Officer Jones – that you are fundamentally wrong. That your mind is focused on some scary idea of a kid out there alone in the dark countryside, and the whole thing is a fucked-up fantasy.'

Leighton started to speak, but the chief held up a hand to stop him again, and he fell silent. 'I get it – clearly you genuinely believe that you saw Tina Blanchette, but you need to accept that is looking increasingly unlikely. If you are unwilling to accept that fact, your future as a cop is in serious jeopardy. As a cop with psychological issues and a reprimand on the record for abandoning your post, you're already on shaky ground.' Winston sighed. 'But I know that all of this may not be enough to move you off this obsession, so you should know something else.'

'What?'

'We got another call from a member of the public confirming that a girl matching Tina's description was seen in a McDonald's just outside the Alaskan state line. She was with a man who she called 'dad', and the witness said she had some type of fairy tattoo on the back of her hand. That's a detail that exactly matches information given to us by Angela Blanchette. It is also one we never shared outside of this investigation.'

Leighton felt like he'd been hit by a freight train.

'I'm sorry, chief. I really don't know what to say.'

'Say you'll let this madness go and get on with doing your job.'

'Yes, sir.' Leighton rubbed the back of his neck. 'I was just so sure.'

'Look, Leighton, you've been through a lot this year, maybe you need to realise that your head will be messed up for a long time. Do you understand that?'

'I guess I'm starting to.'

'Well then go home for the day. Come back in the morning ready to work.'

'Yes, sir,' Leighton nodded.

'And take this shit with you.' He pushed the map across the table to Leighton, who folded it and slipped it into his pocket.

After he was gone, Chief Winston swore under his breath. He was unsure if he could ever get Jones back on track, but for the time being things appeared potentially stable, though that didn't mean it would last. Picking up the sheet of paper, Winston turned it over and took a pen from his shirt pocket. He began filling it in. The form was an S14 Record of Professional Misconduct.

54

The stranger finished laying the six bear traps at various points in the long grass and trees surrounding the buildings. It had been a major effort too. In the early morning, he had driven in as far as he could from the south. The radio had said that many of the roads further north were closed because of spreading wildfires. So, he had bought a map at a gas station and found an old road which brought him within a mile or so of the farm. But that still left him with a lot of walking to do. To avoid burning himself out, he brought the traps in two at a time. They were heavy, but carrying one in each arm kept him equally balanced. It had taken over half an hour to make each trip, but he made decent time.

The spring traps were difficult for one person to prize open, but he had eventually managed without losing any fingers. Now they were lying, like lethal open mouths, half hidden between the trees.

Once the traps were all placed, the stranger dropped a can of soda and candy bar in the centre of each of them. That would hopefully attract the kid. But also let him know where they were.

His plan was to enter each building in turn, flush the kid out. He reckoned she would most likely run into the flat wooded area in front of the buildings rather than up the steep slope behind them. She would foolishly think that she had more chance of escape in the woods.

55

As Leighton walked along the corridor from administration to the locker room, he passed by Danny Clarke who was adjusting his belt in preparation for starting his shift.

'Hey, Danny,' Leighton said, 'you still riding solo?'

'Hell yeah,' Danny said with a wink, 'and it really beats the alternative, if you know what I mean.'

'I hear you, buddy,' Leighton said, trying to look and sound upbeat until Danny had gone.

Leighton then trudged to the locker area. Everything felt wrong. He undid his belt and hung it on a flat hook in his locker. The inside door, which was hanging open, featured a Polaroid photograph of Annie drinking an impossibly large milkshake he had bought at Rubies Diner on the pier. It was a place they both loved to go; where Leighton would watch the tumbling waves, and Annie would look out for the comical pelicans. Leighton instinctively smiled when he saw the photograph. He missed her, but at least she would be home the following evening and that part of his life – the good part – would be complete again. Closing the locker, Leighton sat down in the empty space, ran a hand through his hair. He felt exhausted and emotionally drained. Taking a seat on the low benches, he stared at his feet and sighed.

'Hey, Jonesy.'

Leighton turned around to see Lisa standing in the doorway.

'You look pretty tired there, are you alright?' she asked.

'No not really, the chief just dragged me in for a chat.'

'Was it about the Blanchette kid?' Lisa looked like she already knew the answer to the question.

'Yeah. Looks like I'm wrong about it.'

'Well, I heard they searched everywhere within the area you suggested, even used a helicopter fitted with infra-red and found nothing.'

'Yeah, that's pretty much what I just heard too.'

'So, if they've checked it all out, I suppose that's it finished. You're free to move on – maybe find a new hobby.'

'Yeah, I guess I won't need this anymore.'

Leighton pulled out the crumpled photocopy of the map from his chest pocket and unfolded it. He peered at the map for a moment. Locating the place on the road where he had stopped. He used one fingernail to trace the line from the road to the site of the old farm biting his bottom lip as he stared at the image.

'I got it wrong,' he said, quietly, almost in in whisper. 'They were looking in the wrong damned place.'

'What do you mean?' Lisa asked with a note of concern that was more for Leighton than the missing girl.

'The area they looked at was too far south.'

'Meaning what?'

'When I first looked at the area, I figured she would have followed the slope of the landscape as it ran downwards south towards the coast. But the area the suspect's wrote down lies uphill. I think she must have wanted to be uphill, maybe to be able to see if she was being followed. That's why they couldn't find her in that area!'

Lisa looked at Leighton with a combination of pity and frustration. There seemed no way back from the abyss for him.

'Are you listening to yourself, Leighton? What if you sent another helicopter unit out to your new location and they found nothing there either, what would you say then – they were too far east or too far west? You need to step back from this type of thinking before it destroys you.'

'I can't do that,' Leighton said. 'I can let somebody else down.'

'Well, maybe that says more about you than it does about this case.'

'What's that mean?'

'Look,' Lisa sighed, 'I very much doubt there's a little girl out there waiting to be rescued, but I can see that there's a man in front of me who needs to be a hero, for whatever reason. But that doesn't make it real.'

Leighton was already standing up.

'Whether I'm right or wrong, you never saw me,' Leighton said.

Before Lisa could even respond, he was gone.

56

Tina made a decision. She now accepted that nobody was coming for her. The stranger was the only person who know where she was. That meant she had to rely on herself if she was going to survive. She had been crouched in a corner of one of the four rooms in the office building. From her position she could peer through a hole in the plaster at the stranger who had been arranging something in the woods. When he had finished, he came out of among the trees, whistling while carrying a long-handled axe. He then made his way into the barn.

Tina held her breath and tiptoed through to the main office, which was closest to the barn. From here she had a partial view of the inside. Initially, Tina had thought optimistically that the stranger was going to climb into the pit, but instead he seemed to clamber up on to the platform. At this point he was lost from sight, but Tina heard loud smashing and cracking noises, which told her he was using the axe to smash the platform up. Tina watched in horror as huge planks of wood dropped on the floor and into the central pit. One of them lay across the top of it like the balance beam they used in her school gymnasium.

Finally, when there was nothing remaining of the upper floor of the barn but a thin ledge, the stranger slid down wrecked planks to the floor below. It was then that he appeared to notice something down in the pit.

The stranger seemed to stop moving entirely, as if hypnotised by the sight. The planks he had dropped into the pit created countless new hiding places down there in the darkness. Eventually, he stepped forward and gripped the top of the rusting ladder. Then he began to climb down.

As soon as she saw him descend into the machine pit, Tina crawled through the hole at the back of the office wall and began scrambling barefoot up the slope of the hill.

She made it to the top and had hoped to walk back in the direction she had come four days earlier, but when she reached the top, Tina found herself looking at a very different landscape. The entire area was blanketed in grey smoke. Putting her hand to her mouth, Tina tried in vain to block out the chocking smell of burning wood. In the distance, she could just make out a glowing orange ribbon of fire, flickering crazily on the horizon. This ribbon appeared to be moving rapidly in her direction.

57

When Leighton stepped out of the station building, a yellow cab pulled up and Angela Blanchette climbed out of the shuddering vehicle and hurried over to him. 'Angela, what's going on?' Leighton asked.

'You never got back to me,' she said, frantically, 'so I thought I'd come down and find out what the hell is going on. I can't just sit there and do nothing – it's killing me.'

'I get that.' Leighton nodded. 'Listen, I need you to come with me right now.' Leighton glanced back over his shoulder at the station building.

'Do you know where she is then?' Angela asked.

'I'm not sure – maybe. I think so. But we really need to go now!'

Leighton quickly led Angela to his car, and they both climbed in.

'Where are we going?' she asked.

'Into the country on the north-east of the city.'

'Oh,' was all Angela could say. She felt Leighton's words push against the edge of the protective barrier surrounding her mind. Despite the certainty in Leighton's voice, she almost didn't dare to hope anymore. The last few days had taught her that to hope was very tempting but also dangerous. Hope could easily arrive full of promise and sweetness only to turn sour and leave her more broken than before. And yet this time it seemed different, as if the strength of her belief could somehow restore her lost child.

'Do you really think that–' she began to ask the questions, but her speech was eclipsed by a surge of aching desperation to hold her child again.

Leighton reached across, momentarily placed his hand on hers, and nodded. That was enough for Angela Blanchette who smiled and mouthed a silent plea to the universe.

As they drove out of the station and on to Mission Avenue, Leighton turned to Angela. 'Look, I'm sorry it's taken me so long to join the dots.'

'It's okay,' Angela said, 'you seem to be the only one who tried.'

'Let's just hope I'm right,' Leighton said and floored the gas pedal.

58

Tina slid unsteadily back down the slope, just in time to glimpse the stranger clambering out of the pit into the jagged wreckage of the barn. Luckily, the thickening smoke drifting down the slope served to conceal her from his gaze. She paused and watched as he ran around the place in demented circles.

Unable to return to the relative safety of the barn, Tina limped toward the back wall of the office, but with the fire spreading all around, she knew it was only a matter of time before she ran out of ways to avoid her pursuer.

Creeping along the side of the office wall, Tina listened carefully. When she reached the corner, she glanced around it and saw the stranger. He was standing still and staring into the trees, transfixed as if he had heard something. After a moment he sprinted into the wilderness and vanished.

59

Leighton was driving quickly along the winding road out of the city. If he had been calmer he might have noticed that the roads were much quieter than usual, but his mind was so focused on the road that he almost didn't notice when Angela Blanchette – who had seemed almost catatonic – started to speak.

'I knew life could hurt when David left us,' she said as if to herself, 'we had all been good at the start. Every Friday he would bring me flowers – yellow roses – they were my favourite. But then he stopped doing that and spent more and more time away from me and Tina. It kinda hurt even then, but there was the two of us locked together. And when he left, I reckon I hurt more because of what it meant for Tina than for myself.'

'That must've been tough,' Leighton said.

Angela continued to stare out of the window. 'It felt like a pinprick compared to this,' she said.

'Yeah,' Leighton nodded. 'I can only imagine your pain. My daughter is everything to me.'

'Is she with her mother?'

'No, my wife died sixteen months ago.' Leighton glanced sideways at the road edge to avoid meeting Angela's gaze.

'I'm sorry.'

'You've done nothing wrong. Annie is staying with her grandparents for a couple of days.'

'Will she like that?'

'I think so. They'll spoil her with gifts and make sure she has better food than the pizza and ice cream I give her.'

Angela smiled and Leighton noticed. 'What's funny?' he asked.

'One summer, Tina got a taste for mint choc chip ice cream. She'd tried it a neighbour's house and convinced me to buy her a couple of pints. Anyway, she got up one morning saying she didn't want her breakfast waffles and was too sick for school. When I asked her if she had eaten anything the previous evening she just shrugged. But when I went to throw her breakfast in the trash I found an empty ice-cream carton.'

'Midnight feast?'

'Yep, and she never touched the stuff ever again.' Angela smiled sadly and gazed through her window.

Leighton followed her concerned gaze toward the horizon where thick columns of smoke rose from the surrounding hillsides. Leighton had noticed them too and was glad that, under these particular circumstances, Annie was staying with her grandparents.

'Please hurry,' Angela said. There was no need to explain that if they didn't make it in time, the smoke would be just as effective as any other killer.

'We're almost at the place where I think I saw her,' Leighton said.

Up ahead, a fire officer dressed in tan coloured protective clothing was standing in the middle of the road waving both arms to halt Leighton.

After braking to a stop, Leighton rolled down his driver window as the firefighter approached the car.

'Excuse me, sir, this area is in the red zone; you're going to have to turn around quickly.'

'I'm a cop!' Leighton said as he held up his badge with one hand, 'I really need to get through.'

The fire officer shook his head. 'Doesn't matter if you're the police commissioner, the fire chief told all units that nobody's getting through! The fire is spreading in all directions and we're evacuating all homes in a six-mile radius. This whole place might be ash by morning. So, you have to move out!'

'Fair enough, I guess,' Leighton said with a shrug.

'What?' Angela's eyes widened in horror. She turned and stared at Leighton in disbelief.

'Okay,' the fire officer said as he tapped the roof of the car, 'you can turn around here and head back the way you came. Most roads back to the city should be clear.'

'Sure, thanks,' Leighton said and rolled up his window.

'What the hell!' Angela looked at Leighton with tears in her eyes. However, rather than say anything, he simply reversed his car at ninety degrees until it was facing the exact spot where Tina had vanished five days earlier, then accelerated as fast as he could into the countryside.

The roar of Leighton's engine caused the fire officer who had been walking away to turn around. His eyes widened in horror, and he attempted to run after the vehicle, but it had already been swallowed by a wave of white smoke.

The car shuddered and clattered as Leighton drove through the smoky landscape. Bushes had caught in his wheels, making a sound like dried fingers scratching on the underside of the car.

'Look at the map,' Leighton said as he reached into his pocket and pushed the folded piece of paper towards Angela. 'Look at this. You see that area circled in red?'

Angela unfolded the map and then nodded.

'Well that's a place I found written down in Craven's trailer. It's too much of a coincidence that he'd be writing the name of a place that's so close to where I saw Tina. If Tina's not with him – and I don't think she is – then I figure that's where he thinks she is.'

'How far is it?'

'Ten – fifteen minutes, maybe. Depends if this smoke thins out a bit.'

'How would she have gotten so far out here?' Angela asked.

'Walked most probably. I think he had her in his car, was driving towards his trailer, and she escaped somehow. This is where she ran to.'

Hot tears began to slide down Angela's face as she thought of her small, scared daughter alone in this place. Her emotional pain and sense of guilt was so strong that it threatened to overwhelm her, but it was, of course, eclipsed by another thought – one that gave her power rather than took it from her. Angela Blanchette imagined what she would do to the man who did this to her child.

'Hopefully the spreading fires mean that Craven won't still be in the area and we can focus on finding Tina.'

'I hope he is still around,' Angela said with a voice that Leighton barely recognised.

***

Leighton and Angela continued driving through drifting pockets of smoke until eventually they found themselves at the bottom of a tree covered slope. Leighton slammed on the brakes, knowing that the trees were too close together for the car to fit through. The car lurched to a stop.

'We'll have to walk from here,' Leighton said, but as he turned to see if that was okay with Angela, he discovered she was already climbing out of the vehicle.

Hurrying after Angela into the hazy wilderness, Leighton had to brace himself against the choking smoke that was thickening around them. He caught up with Angela who was coughing loudly as she scrambled up the dusty slope.

'The air should be clearer at the top,' he said.

Angela nodded, and together they made their way up the crumbling slope.

Leighton's theory proved to be correct – the air seemed to clear as he and Angela neared the top of the ridge. It was as they reached the summit that Leighton and Angela found themselves looking down on the cluster of old orchard buildings. The hill they stood upon curved around either side of them like a crescent moon.

'I think we should split up and take a side each,' Angela said.

'We'd be safer together.'

'She could be on either side,' Angela said. 'If we split up then we have a better chance of finding her.' What Angela did not say was that if Tina was dead, then she didn't want anyone else to be there if she found her. That would be her undoing and she couldn't face that with an audience. In her back pocket was a packet of pills. If it turned out that Tina was there, and she was dead, Angela did not intend to return from this trip.

'Okay.' Leighton nodded. 'But I want you to take this.' He reached to his holster and realised in horror that he had left his utility belt and gun back in his locker.

'Shit! I've no gun.' Leighton kicked at the dry ground.

'It's okay,' Angela said. 'I'm going anyway.'

'Well, you shout out if you see anything. Okay?'

Angela nodded and then vanished down the slope. She wasn't even thinking, but Leighton couldn't blame her. He would be exactly the same in that situation.

60

Angela had been clumsily descending the slope through the trees when she noticed something familiar lying in the dust. Tina's blue canvas sandal half concealed in a small ditch. Stifling a sob, she fell to the ground and reached for it.

As she turned the small sandal over in her hands, hot tears scorched Angela Blanchette's cheeks. The shoe had her daughter's name and class neatly printed inside in case it got mixed up at school. Angela held on to it as if it were the most precious thing in the world. She felt as if the universe was somehow rewarding her for her belief.

'Leighton. I've found something,' she called through the smoky air. 'My baby was here! You hear me, Leighton? She could still be alive'

'Not for long,' said a voice from directly behind her.

Angela turned around quickly, but was not quite fast enough to avoid the sudden blow to her face, which sent her tumbling into darkness.

Edward Craven grinned as he stepped over the woman's motionless body. For a moment he considered dragging her down to one of the nearby traps and springing it on her leg, but he was interrupted by the sound of Leighton calling Tina's name from somewhere nearby. Glancing back at the woman, he saw that her eyes had rolled back like white marbles, indicating she was unconscious. The smoke from the fires was thickening all around. He therefore tore the sandal from Angela's hand and hurried in the direction in which she had been yelling.

By the time Leighton had heard Angela's muffled voice calling, he was already down on level ground. As he moved through the trees, he narrowly avoided stepping on to a sprung trap, which sat like a shark's mouth beneath a tree. The tree was cut in half, as if somebody had taken an axe to it for hours on end. He figured whoever had attacked the tree and set the trap was clearly very dangerous. Stepping cautiously out of the tree line, Leighton found himself standing in the patch of dry ground between the office building, a long wooden building and what appeared to be an abandoned picnic. Cupping his hands to his mouth, he called Tina's name again, but the smoke drifting into the area had made his throat hoarse. Glancing up at the slope above the buildings, he could already see the first hungry tongues of flame licking at the trees on the ridge. He knew that if he didn't get Angela out of there soon, they most probably would never leave.

'Tina!' he called again into the thickening air. There was no response and, in the silence, Leighton became aware of another sound. It was a deep roaring sound that reminded him of a waterfall or fast flowing water. In a moment of lucidity, he realised it was the sound of the approaching fire.

Leighton called one last time, and he was almost ready to leave when he saw her.

A small, skinny seven year old, in a dirty orange T-shirt and shorts was standing in the remains of the crumbling barn and looking directly at him. Leighton felt his heart jump with fright.

'Hey there, Tina, it's okay,' he said. The girl vanished back into the vast structure.

Leighton hurried after her into the darkness. When his eyes adjusted to the gloom, he found the girl, but her location made her impossible to reach. The upper floor of the building looked as if it had collapsed. In the middle of the barn floor was a huge pit, which appeared to contain some rusting old machinery. Stretching out over the top of this abyss was a long plank of wood. Tina Blanchette was standing on this beam, like a tiny pirate being made to walk the plank. Tina's body looked frozen with fear. Leighton worried that any movement could spook her and send her tumbling into the pit below. Without moving at all, Leighton looked at the kid and smiled.

'It's okay, Tina,' Leighton said, quietly.

'I want my mom,' Tina said, her eyes wide and scared.

'She came here with me,' Leighton said, 'she'll be here soon.'

'He's lying.' The words caused Tina to turn around and find the stranger standing on the opposite side of the barn.

'Don't listen to him,' Leighton called.

'If your mom was with him, she'd be here wouldn't she, but she's not.'

In that moment, Leighton realised that there was certainty in the other man's voice. That meant he had already found Angela – and therefore likely killed her. A feeling of panic flooded his stomach, but he knew he couldn't lose focus or he would lose Tina too.

'She's with me, honey,' Leighton said, 'she has been speaking about you all the way up here. She told me you once liked mint choc ice cream and that you once finished a whole carton of it, then had a tummy ache for a whole night.'

A smile touched the edges of Tina's mouth. She took a small step towards Leighton.

'Hey, Tina,' the stranger called. 'I told you he was dangerous. He probably hurt your mom to make her tell him those things.'

Tina glanced back at him, her eyes wide in horror.

'Yeah,' he continued, gleefully, 'he probably sneaked into your house at night and cut her until she told him those things.'

'That's not true,' Leighton said, softly, 'you know that's not true. He's just a sick man who's saying those things to scare you into doing what he wants. I bet that's how he got you to go with him from the creek. Maybe he told you that you were in danger or that your mom was – something to scare you, didn't he?'

Tina looked at him, but her expression gave nothing away.

'That's a lie!' the stranger called, but this time Tina did not turn back around. She knew that it wasn't.

'You can trust me, Tina. Look, I brought this for you,' Leighton said, softly, as he reached into his trouser pocket and pulled out the small plastic poodle.

'He's not the good one! He's a liar!' the stranger screamed.

For a moment, Leighton remained silent. He glanced to the side and then swallowed visibly. When his eyes met those of the child again, something had shifted in them.

'He's right,' Leighton said, softly, 'I'm not a good person.' Hot tears slid down his cheeks as he spoke but he seemed unconcerned. 'I've made mistakes – Tina – stupid ones.'

'Like what?' the girl asked.

'Well,' Leighton swallowed, 'I guess I let somebody who I loved drift away from me until she was so far away I couldn't ever reach her. That hurt her and it hurt my baby girl. I know I'm not a good person, Tina, but because of my mistakes, I want to be better – as a dad, as a cop – maybe just as a person. So, I'm trying to be a good person. If I can help somebody, I will try. That's why I'm here for you right now. The other cops wouldn't come looking for you. They thought you were maybe up in Alaska with your dad, but I refused to give up on you. Do you understand that?'

The girl nodded as she stared intently at the small piece of yellow plastic in Leighton's hand.

'You know, I found this the night you ran in front of my car,' he said, quietly. 'You dropped it when my car gave you a fright didn't you?'

Tina glanced up at his face and something softened in her expression. She nodded. It was a small gesture, just visible enough for Leighton to notice.

'I'm sorry I couldn't find you then. But I want you to know that I came back to look for you. By then you had already gone. This was on the ground, and I knew how important it would be to you because my own little girl has one just like it, with a tiny plastic bowl too. The tail on her one broke off too, but she doesn't mind.'

'He's a fuckin liar!' the stranger screeched, his voice cracking with emotion. Leighton ignored the interruption, keeping his tired eyes fixed on the small girl's face.

'If you trust me, I'll take you to your mom. She's the one who can really keep you safe – not some scary man. Okay?'

Tina's small tired eyes revealed her exhaustion and confusion. She didn't know what to do.

'He's telling the truth, baby,' a croaky voice called out from over Leighton's shoulder. He turned his head to see Angela, her eyes barely open and a ruby trickle of blood staining her forehead. She was standing upright but gripping the barn door frame for support.

The sight of her mom, bleeding but alive, was too much for Tina. She suddenly stepped across the creaking beam to Leighton who scooped her up his arms and stumbled from the barn into a fog of dense choking smoke.

Behind him, the stranger roared and snorted in rage. It was inconceivable that the kid did not fall for his technique. Possessed with a sudden need to slaughter them all, he pulled his hunting knife from a buckskin sheath on his belt. He then hurried towards the beam that Tina had deftly crossed. However, as he tried stepping forwards – putting his weight on the narrow plank – he heard the dry crack of breaking wood.

'Fuck!' he roared, as he stared down at the twelve-foot drop that would surely see him landing atop a group of rusty pipes. He steadied himself, then turned and ran through the rear of the dusty barn. Racing around the side of the smouldering building, he moved in the same direction as Leighton but by the time he stepped outside, the stranger discovered that the cop and the kid had vanished. He spun around looking jerkily in every direction, but the smoke from the encroaching fire was blocking any sunlight. Even the farm buildings were melting into the expanding grey void. He realised then that he now had three witnesses who would provide a compelling case to any jury. If he allowed any of them to survive, his fate would be sealed, and he had heard how child killers were treated in jail.

'I'm going to find you!' he screamed into the dense white air, 'I'm going to fucking skin all three of you!'

Craven tilted his head and listened like a demented dog. From somewhere nearby, he heard the muffled sound of a child coughing. Grinning to himself, Craven broke into a run, following the sound into the smoke where he was soon consumed in the white drifting madness.

Leaping over fallen trees he followed the sound of sporadic coughing through the smoke. Pulling his T-shirt collar up over his mouth and nose, he leapt around the woods – blade in hand – like some ghost from the frontier. He stopped every few paces, when his head twitched from side to side as he listened intently for his prey. It was difficult to distinguish the sound of footfalls from twigs cracking in the escalating heat. Eventually, however, he heard another cough, and locked his head on to the direction of the sound. With the encroaching fire pressing in on all sides, he raced after the sound of the girl coughing.

Leaping through the maze of dried trees, Craven was easily able to catch up with the cop, who was slowed by the weight of the kid and the stumbling of her semi-conscious mother. Within moments, the killer appeared a few feet in front of Leighton and Angela. He was barely visible in the billowing thick smoke that was filling the area. A smile flickered across his face. As Leighton looked desperately from side to side.

It was clear to everyone that carrying the sleeping bundle that was Tina made it impossible for the cop to escape. For once in his life, Leighton wished he had a gun.

'I told you, I'd find you,' Craven called out with a wide, self-satisfied smile.

'I'm sorry,' Leighton said to Angela while he kept his eyes fixed on Craven.

'You should be,' Craven said, gleefully. 'You brought her here to this place to die in the dirt.'

Leighton turned around in the hope of finding an escape but still held fast to the child. The fact that their attacker stood only a few feet away made escape impossible. In the smoky gloom, with his wild appearance, Craven looked entirely like the stuff of nightmares. His clothes were streaked with mud and ash, only his eyes and teeth stood out in the shadows. In his right hand he held the long knife. His skinny arms were scratched and bleeding. The hand gripping the long blade was trembling with a combination of excitement and rage.

It was then that Leighton noticed the split tree slightly to Craven's left.

'Angela,' he said, softly, 'I need you to move with me, okay?'

Tina's mother nodded.

Leighton carried the child two steps to one side.

'Hey, where you off to?' Craven called out. 'That's pathetic. I already told you – time's up!'

'Take another step,' Leighton whispered.

Angela moved, and still with the child in his arms, Leighton moved too.

'You're not going fucking anywhere!' Craven roared and lurched through the trees towards Leighton who instinctively turned around to shield Tina with his body.

There was a sudden loud cracking noise followed by a guttural scream. In the haze of thickening smoke, Leighton turned his head to see the stranger thrashing around on the ground. Even from where he stood, Leighton could see that Craven's left leg had been snapped in the bear trap which now gripped it like a piece of meat in a vice.

'Fucking help me,' Craven screeched, 'for God's sake.' His eyes were bulging and veins stuck out on his neck like fleshy tendrils. He desperately attempted to shift his body, and screamed again as the crushed fragments of bone grated against each other.

Even if he hadn't been carrying Tina, Leighton still would not have prevented Angela Blanchette from doing what she did next.

Stepping forward, in an almost dreamlike way, she picked up the knife that Craven had dropped. The one he hoped to use on her and her child.

'Take her out of here, please,' she said to Leighton.

Leighton looked at her for a moment and then nodded. He hoisted Tina up on to his shoulder and ran, stumbling and looking out for traps, in the direction where the smoke looked least dense. Eventually he found himself standing on a dusty plain devoid of trees.

Moments later, Angela burst out of the trees behind Leighton. She was no longer carrying the knife.

'Look,' he pointed to the burning slope behind them. 'I guess we can't go back over the hill now,' Leighton said.

But Angela wasn't listening; she was only concerned with stroking her daughter's hair.

'We need to find the car,' Leighton said, 'if it's torched already we'll have a long walk south. Can you manage that?'

'I can manage anything now,' Angela said. 'Thank you, Leighton.'

'Hey, save it till we are out of this barbecue,' Leighton said as he adjusted Tina on his shoulder. 'Let's go!'

They skirted around the edge of the hill and discovered that the direction of the spreading fire – which had cut across the entire hill at an angle – had spared Leighton's car. The entire slope of the hill above it had been reduced to black stubble. Leighton's sense of relief was clearly visible on his face. Angela thought it was because now they could all go home, but in actual fact Leighton's joy was because of his car's connection to the people he loved.

Moving carefully, Leighton helped Angela into the back seat, where Tina – who was only half awake – refused to let her mom go. Leighton stretched a safety belt across the pair of them.

As the car bounced back over the charred and dusty landscape, Leighton tried to drive as carefully as he could. To the western side of the car he could see fire-planes swooping in above the hillsides to drop a slow pink mist onto the spreading flames. The misty falling water in the air was almost hypnotic.

'Leighton,' Angela said.

'Yeah?'

'There's no rush.'

'Sorry,' he said, 'it's just this surface is a bit crazy.'

'No, I mean, I'm quite happy here like this.' She glanced down at her sleeping child. 'I had nothing, and you gave me everything back. Thank you – for everything.'

'You're welcome,' Leighton said, softly, and for a moment he almost liked himself.

61

Leighton drove into the parking lot of Oceanside Police Station. This time he used the area at the front of the building. It seemed to Leighton, upon returning from the vast scorched landscape of Pembleton Farm, that the peach coloured building on Mission Avenue was somehow smaller.

He had only just got out of the car when Chief Winston slammed the glass door of the station open and rushed out of the building. As he strode towards Leighton, his eyes were hidden in a maze of angry lines.

'Jones, where the fuck have you been?' he barked. 'I got a report from the owner of the Four Winds Trailer Park of a break-in to one of his trailers, the licence plate he gave matches yours. Then I hear from the fire commissioner who states that you deliberately entered into an active hot zone in the middle of the wildfires. What the hell is wrong with you?'

'Sorry, chief,' Leighton said, calmly, 'I went looking for Tina, but it's okay because—'

'Shut the hell up! I don't want to hear any more of your madness!' Winston interrupted and held up his hand to silence the younger officer.

'But sir—' Leighton tried.

'Enough, Jones, I mean it! You're a pretty good cop. God knows you've had your personal and professional problems and that's the reason I've been accommodating to you.'

'I appreciate that, sir.'

'Then why would an officer in your situation disobey a direct order?'

'I don't know,' Leighton shrugged, 'I just had a feeling.'

'You had a feeling?'

'Okay, it was more than that – a hunch or instinct – something like that.'

'Christ, man, you're a fucking traffic cop, not a Coney Island psychic.'

'I know,' Leighton looked at his feet, 'I'm sorry, sir.'

'Well, that's of little consequence; I have no choice but to suspend you pending investigation into gross misconduct.'

'Oh, come on, chief, that's half pay. You can't be serious? I've got bills to pay.'

'And the worst part is this, Jones,' Winston pointed an assertive finger a Leighton's chest, 'that whilst your skipping about the Oceanside backwoods with a flashlight, the little kid is most likely sitting pretty in Alaska with her daddy.'

'You're wrong, sir,' Leighton said with a sigh, 'I'm not accepting suspension. I can't.'

'Stop speaking, officer.' Winston appeared as if he was about to combust.

'Don't you even want to know what I discovered out there?' Leighton asked.

'Don't start again with this bull, Jones. You're the one who's wrong. I don't want to hear another word or that suspension will become permanent. With a kid to raise on your own, you need to be a hell of a lot more responsible.'

'Sir, with all due respect, you're way out of line.'

'Jesus! Okay, I'm done with this shit. Jones, you're fired!'

'What?' Leighton frowned in shock, his thoughts were scrambled in a mixture of confusion and disbelief.

'You heard me. And you brought this shit down on your own head. I told you that your wild turkey hunt for the kid was a fucking waste of time, but no – you had to go follow your half-assed instinct. Well, I guess now you'll have a hell of a lot more free time to spend wandering around the countryside in search of the kid.'

With his authority asserted, Chief Winston adjusted his tie then turned and walked back towards the glass doors of the station. He had almost reached them when he heard a woman's voice call from behind him.

'Excuse me, chief!' she called out across the baking heat of the station parking lot. Winston slowly turned around to see Angela Blanchette standing next to Leighton Jones. The woman looked exhausted, scraped and bruised and yet capable of fighting off the entire world if she had to. In contrast, the grubby child sleeping in her arms looked blissfully calm with one sweaty arm curled instinctively around her mother's neck.

'My name is Angela Claire Blanchette, and I would just like to confirm,' she said in a voice which was hoarse from endless nights of calling into the darkness for her lost child, 'that – with the help of this good man here – my baby girl is no longer missing. Some sick bastard had taken her, just like I said.'

Chief Winston looked suddenly pale. 'Miss, I don't–'

This time it was Leighton's turn to hold up a hand and silence the chief.

'Don't bother, chief. Mrs Blanchette probably wants to sign the paperwork and get her kid safely home. Given that instead of relaxing in Alaska, Tina spent several nights scared and alone on a deserted orchard hiding from a deranged killer, I'd imagine that she needs to get home for a bath and some decent food.'

'There are still procedures to go through,' Winston said, but his voice was less authoritative.

'Well, maybe some of those medical checks can be done at home just as easily,' Leighton said as he led Angela and Tina past Chief Winston and towards the entrance of the police station.

***

An hour later, despite Leighton's optimism, both Tina and her mother had been taken to the Tri City Medical Centre for an examination. A couple of units had been dispatched to the Old

Mill Way site, but the spreading fire made it impossible to get anywhere near the old farm.

In the meantime, standard protocol meant that Leighton had been required to submit a written report. So, he had dutifully taken the triplicate form to the area of the station shared by traffic and general crime.

Slumping into a seat, Leighton had only started filling in his form when he became aware of a presence standing over him. He glanced up and realised it was Captain Pierce.

'Thank you very fucking much, Jones,' he said.

Leighton glanced up. He had expected some fallout from the incident, but Pierce looked enraged.

'What's your problem, captain? The kid's alive. I thought you'd be pleased.'

'Pleased? You deliberately fucked up an investigation of another team, for your own personal glory and pissed off my boss.'

'That's not true.' Leighton pointed an accusative finger back at Pierce. 'I tried to hand everything I had to anybody else who might listen. But nobody would – not you or Levvy or the chief.'

'Well, I hope you're happy that you deliberately made your colleagues, Officers Dane and Lorenzo, look incompetent.'

'Hey, those two did that all by themselves.'

'Man, I'm just glad I'm moving on from this shithole!'

'You and me both,' Leighton said with a wry smile.

'You're going to get yourself fired if you don't watch that attitude.'

'Maybe,' Leighton shrugged, 'but not twice in the same day. Even I'm not that special.'

Pierce turned to go, but couldn't leave without throwing a final curveball. 'I'll be sure to remind Gretsch to keep you on a tight leash.'

'Who the hell is Gretsch?' Leighton asked.

'Your new boss as of next Tuesday. Oh, and starting Monday you've got a new partner – Danny Clarke. Try to do a better job of getting along with him than you did with the last one.'

With those parting words, Pierce turned on his heels and left.

Leighton finished his report with a smile on his face; Tina was safe and Angela had her child back. It was also good to know that Pierce was leaving, and that Teddy was no longer on his back. There was also comfort to be found in the fact that he would now have a dependable partner in Danny Clarke, but knowing that Tina was safe and that his own little girl would be returning home was more than enough to lift Leighton's spirits.

Epilogue

Leighton picked up the telephone and held it to his ear for a moment. He then felt a sudden sense of doubt and quickly returned it to the cradle. It seemed ridiculous that he would be so affected by the thought of asking somebody to dinner. And yet, standing in the doorway between his kitchen and living room, he felt like an excited teenager trying to summon the courage to ask for a prom date. But it was perhaps because he liked Angela so much, that the situation felt much more pressured than it had to be.

Unable to face the prospect of a telephone exchange in which he would be unable to read Angela's facial expressions, Leighton decided on a different course of action. Moving into the kitchen he opened a drawer packed with paperwork. After rummaging around, he pulled out the white-paged book and laid it on the kitchen counter. After thumbing through the thin pages for a moment, he eventually stopped, folded back a page corner and carried the book back to the telephone. Leighton picked up the handset and punched in the numbers.

Holding the phone to his ear he waited for a moment, and glanced anxiously around his small living room. There was a click and a cheerful voice answered.

'Hello, Floral Fantastic. How may I help you today?'

'Hi,' Leighton said, softly, 'I'd like to order some flowers, yellow roses if you have them.'

'Is that a bouquet or an arrangement?'

'I don't know,' Leighton felt a moment of panic, 'what would you suggest?'

'Well, are the flowers for collection or delivery?'

'Delivery, I'd like them sent to her house.'

'Then a bouquet would be nice.'

'Thank you,' Leighton said with an audible sense of relief.

'What would you like the card to say?'

'The card?'

'Yes, we place them in with the flowers, to let the recipient know who sent them.'

There was a moment's silence while Leighton considered this.

'You don't have to include your name, just a message.'

'That would be better,' Leighton said.

'Okay – we have standard bouquets at twenty-five dollars or luxury ones at forty-five.'

'Luxury, please.'

'And you want all yellow roses?'

'Yes.'

'Okay, and what would you like the message to be?'

'Can it be, "I miss hanging around you, call me sometime."'

***

Having placed his order, Leighton had some other unfinished business to arrange before Annie got back home. He drove across the city, stopping off only once at the supermarket to pick up some groceries, but before returning home, he pulled into the parking lot of Sunbeam Garden Retirement Village.

This time when he entered the brightly-coloured reception; the young man he had previously met was engrossed in replacing a black ink cartridge.

'Hi,' Leighton said, 'I don't mean to disturb you. I just want to leave something for one of the residents.' Leighton placed the bottle of Jim Beam Bourbon on the counter.

'No problem,' the young man said, brightly, as he wiped his stained fingers on a white cloth. 'Now which guest is it for?'

'Len Wells,' Leighton said. 'I was here visiting him on Wednesday.'

'Oh,' the young man's expression conveyed the situation without the need for words, 'I'm afraid Mr Wells passed away yesterday morning. Didn't you hear?'

Leighton was knocked off balance.

'No, I'm not a relative. I'm a cop and he was an ex-cop. I came to him for advice.'

'Ah, he was very ill. I understand he had refused treatment. Said it would be better if the medicine was used on someone younger than him. He used bourbon for the pain.'

'Poor guy,' Leighton said.

'After you left the other day, Len called up reception and said you had left something behind. He got Laura who was working that evening to go over and get it. Do you know what it was?'

'No,' Leighton couldn't remember leaving anything.

'Hang on,' the young man said, 'I'll check.' He then vanished into the back office for a moment and returned a moment later with the black box file. Leighton recognised it as the one containing Len's case notes.

'He's written *Mr Jones* on the top of it. I take it that's you?' the young man asked.

'Yes. Sorry, I must've forgotten to lift it when I left.'

As Leighton walked back to the car with Len's box file in one hand a bottle of Jim Beam in the other, he felt like he had inherited the essence of someone else's life… or mantel.

***

It was more than a week later when Leighton decided to raise his game a little with Angela. Partly, it was because Annie was seeming to be increasingly independent, but also because since meeting Angela Blanchette, he had realised that there were plenty more hurt and lonely people out there. It didn't seem right that they shouldn't find some company.

He knew he still had the toy dog to return to Tina. Perhaps if he dropped it off personally, he could invite Angela and her daughter to dinner. Deciding to take his therapist's advice and shape his own reality, Leighton made a call and booked the table for the following evening at Ruby's on the Pier; a cheerful diner where the girls would hopefully be entertained by the view of the ocean and the greedy pelicans. It was a relaxing place where the adults could talk for a while.

Leighton figured that, rather than facing the discomfort of calling on the telephone, he could drive around to Angela's and then casually invite her and Tina to join him and Annie for something to eat. If they already had plans, it wouldn't be a big deal. He hoped they could agree to reschedule, but at least it would be progress.

***

Annie was sitting in her striped booster seat – happily reading a picture book – when Leighton pulled up his car in the dusty street outside the Blanchette home. He switched off the engine, took a deep breath and then turned in his seat to face his daughter. As he gazed at her small feet tilting from side to side while she peered at the pages, Leighton felt a wave of pure affection wash over him.

'You okay back there, scout?' he asked, half turned in his seat.

'Uh-huh,' Annie said then glanced up from her book to gaze around her at the unfamiliar location.

'Why are we at this place, Daddy?' she asked.

'I just want to say hi to a friend,' Leighton said with a half-suppressed smile. 'It'll just take a moment. I was thinking that maybe I could ask her if she wants to come have dinner with us.'

'Why?' Annie looked at him intently.

'Well, she's had a tough time recently, and she's really nice.'

'What kind of tough time, is she sick?'

'No, she couldn't find her daughter. I helped her.'

'Did you find her?' Annie asked.

'Yes.'

'Good!'

'So, would you be okay with me asking her to dinner?'

Annie shrugged, nodded her head, and returned her attention to her picture book.

'Great. You happy to wait in the car?'

Annie nodded again without looking up.

'Okay, I'll just be standing at that porch,' Leighton said, then climbed out of the vehicle.

The early evening air was cooler than in recent days. As he crossed the small yard, Leighton realised that summer was coming to an end. He glanced back to wave at Annie in the car, but she was too engrossed in the book to require any type of reassurance.

Turning back to face the house, Leighton wondered if the gesture of sending flowers had perhaps been too much. But by the time he reached the door, it was too late to regret anything.

After pressing the small doorbell, he stood nervously for a moment, glancing down at his scuffed boots. He tried rubbing them briefly on the back of each leg, but it had little effect.

When the door eventually opened, Leighton found himself looking at Angela's fresh face and smiling. She was wearing a faded Harley Davidson T-shirt and a pair of denim shorts. A small crusty scrape on her forehead was the only indication of the horror she and Leighton had faced together.

'Wow, Leighton!' she said. 'What a nice surprise. Do you want to come in?'

'Thanks, but I can't,' Leighton said, 'I've got Annie in the car. I just wanted to stop by and return this.'

He held out a hand upon which sat the small plastic dog. He had taken the liberty of dipping it in his kitchen sink and washing away the dust. Now the toy looked as good as new.

'Oh, that's great – Tina will be so happy.' Annie took the toy from Leighton's hand, and the momentary touch of her fingers felt like a small electric shock.

'I think it's the right one,' Leighton said with a half-smile. 'If not, Annie will certainly let me know at some point.'

Angela looked at Leighton with an expression of clear affection, and he knew that he would take this opportunity to ask her if she'd like to join him for dinner. But she spoke first.

'I'm so glad you stopped by, Leighton,' Angela said with a sense of genuine warmth in her voice.

'You are?' Leighton felt a flicker of excitement in his chest.

'Yeah, I'm just so grateful to you,' Angela said. 'And do you know what the best thing is?'

'What?' Leighton smiled, self-consciously.

'Well,' Angela brushed her hair behind one ear, 'you remember me telling you about the yellow roses.'

'Yeah,' Leighton felt himself blush, and glanced momentarily back at his car where Annie remained lost in her small book of happy-ever-after endings.

Angela, who was oblivious to this, carried on talking excitedly.

'So last Friday, Tina and I got back from the mall to find a whole bunch of them. They'd been delivered while we were out and so the driver must've just let them here on the porch. After all this time. Can you believe it?'

'Did you like them?' Leighton asked, cautiously.

'I loved them!' Angela Blanchette's eyes sparkled with delight as she spoke. 'They were yellow – the kind he used to bring me. As soon as I saw them, I knew straight away that Tina's dad must have sent them – you know, when he heard what had happened.'

'But, how–' Leighton tried to form some words, but Angela's enthusiasm propelled her explanation forward.

'So I called him up straight away – and – can you believe it, he flew straight down here on Sunday.'

'Oh, wow,' Leighton said. He felt as if he had been punched in the stomach.

'Yeah, isn't it amazing? We're going to try and work things out. So, I guess you didn't just save Tina; you pretty much saved our entire family.' Angela held his gaze for a moment, and Leighton could see the sincerity and happiness in her expression.

'Dinner's ready!' called a male voice from somewhere back in the restored Blanchette home.

'I'm really happy for you,' Leighton said and glanced down at his feet, 'for all of you. Listen, I best be going, I've got a little table booked for me and Annie down at the harbour.'

'That sounds nice, but don't you want to come in and speak to Tina and David. Both of them would love to see you?'

'No,' Leighton shook his head, 'it's okay. Thank you. I don't want to intrude, and you've all been through enough. But hey, you look after yourself, okay. You've got a second chance to fix things here. Not many folks ever get that.'

Angela nodded. 'It's thanks to you.'

She then took a small step out of the doorway, leaned forward and kissed Leighton gently on the cheek.

'See you around, Leighton Jones,' Angela Blanchette said and then vanished back inside her home.

Leighton turned and walked back to his car, feeling like he was carrying a burden.

As he climbed into his car Leighton sighed and used one hand to massage the back of his neck. Annie glanced up from her book, the turned her face toward the house. When she returned her attention to her book, Leighton thought Annie had been distracted. He was wrong.

'Isn't the lady coming too?' she asked, as she traced her finger over the picture of the rose covered, fairy tale cottage in front of her.

'No, kiddo,' Leighton said as he pulled the car away from the Blanchette family home. 'I'm afraid not.'

After looking at her book of fairy tales for a moment, Annie glanced up at her dad. 'You're just like the woodsman,' she said with a sympathetic tone.

'Huh?' Leighton slowed the car and glanced in the rear-view mirror. 'What d' you mean?'

'In the story, he saved Little Red Riding Hood. At the end she had her family, but the woodsman was just left alone. It's sad.'

'Ah, but I'm not alone, because I've got you.'

'And I've got you too,' Annie smiled, proudly.

'Just you and me, kid,' Leighton said with an affirmative nod of his head.

'That's good, right?' Annie frowned.

'Yeah, I believe it is,' Leighton said. 'You fancy going down to the pier for dinner tonight?'

'For pizza and ice cream?' she asked, excitedly.

'Sure.'

'Then tomorrow we can go to see some birds at the rescue centre?'

'Yeah, why not.'

Leighton, knowing how much Annie loved fluffy birds, conceded and decided that if anyone deserved his love and consideration, it was his daughter.

'Yes!' Annie shouted with joy and for a moment the simple infectious happiness of his daughter was – at least for a while – enough for Leighton Jones.

The car, containing the man and his small daughter moved slowly off, away from the Blanchette family home, and towards a sun that was already steadily sinking behind the silhouette of some distant black mountain.